Last Season At The Halfmoon

Hayden showed me the headline, his face—his father's face—a mask of sorrow. The Halfmoon is important to him. It's where Brad told us he had to leave and where, when he does get back to visit, the three of us go to try to remain a family.

Brad Mackey, just like my father, is a wonderful man— warm, giving, funny and as sexy as it is possible for a man to be. But he's a wanderer, someone who can't stay in one place.

We've managed to stay friends and an odd kind of family for the past six years, mostly—I swear this is true—because of the drive-in. It gave us somewhere to be intimate without being alone. So we didn't have to talk about the oddities of our relationship, about how much Hayden missed his daddy, and we *never* had to talk about whether we missed each other.

I couldn't.

Kate Austin

Kate Austin has worked as a legal assistant, a commercial fisher, a brewery manager, a teacher, a technical writer and a herring popper, while managing to read an average of a book a day. Go ahead—ask her anything. If she doesn't know the answer she'll make it up, because she's been reading and writing fiction for as long as she can remember.

She blames her mother and her two grandmothers for her reading-and-writing obsession—all of them were avid readers and they passed the books and the obsession on to her. She lives in Vancouver, Canada, where she can walk on the beach whenever necessary, even in the rain.

She'd be delighted to hear from readers through her Web site, www.kateaustin.ca.

Last Night
at the Halfmoon

KATE AUSTIN

LAST NIGHT AT THE HALFMOON

copyright ©2007 by Kate Austin

isbn-13:978-0-373-88133-8

isbn-10:   0-373-88133-9

TheNextNovel.com

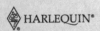 HARLEQUIN®

PRINTED IN U.S.A.

From the Author

Dear Reader,

As you can probably tell from the subject of this book, I'm a movie addict.

But this book began in a way that had nothing to do with movies. I was coming home from Seattle along the I-5, gazing out the window as I do when I take the bus, enjoying every minute of having nothing that I could be doing, when I spotted a decrepit drive-in theater standing guard over a very small town.

That thirty-second glimpse got me thinking—about movies, about drive-ins, about families, about life in a small town. I remembered going to the drive-in as a kid and how much we enjoyed it. I remembered going to the drive-in as a teenager and even as an adult, but now, in my neighborhood, there are no drive-ins.

And that got me thinking about how life in that small town would change when the drive-in closed and how Aimee's life—because she came to me the minute I started thinking about this book—would be transformed forever by this event.

For those of you who might be looking for more information about these movies, www.imdb.com is the best movie database on the Internet. I couldn't have done the research for this book without it.

I'd love to hear from you through my Web site— www.kateaustin.ca.

Kate

To movie lovers everywhere.

CHAPTER 1

La Dolce Vita

My name is unusual, especially here on the West Coast, where very few of us speak French, even as a second language. But I've learned to live with the bungled pronunciation, the questions and the raised eyebrows.

The story, which I've perfected over the years, is both simple and complicated at the same time.

It begins, as has every important event in my life, at the Halfmoon Drive-In in Halfmoon Bay on the Sunshine Coast, just north of Vancouver. It's a place accessible only by water even though it's on the mainland, which might account for a lot of things.

And when I say *every* event, I'm not kidding. My mother tells me I was conceived at the drive-in, and I believe her.

So the story begins.

I was born in April of 1962, nine months almost to the day after the drive-in opened and six months after my parents were married in the registry office on the mainland.

They're happy—happier than most I'd have to say. I still want their relationship to be dark and dramatic—a feeling left over from my teenage years—but it's not. They're romantic comedy, *not* drama.

While I am a foreign film, something indecipherable and gloomy, in black and white rather than color. I like to say that I'm different and I want to be.

My name is Aimee Anouk King, pronounced as "Amy" by everyone except my best friend, T.J.; my ex-husband, Brad, and my parents. I'm named after Anouk Aimee, though I suspect—based on my dad's current movie preferences—he would rather have named me Gidget.

I see my mom's fine hand in my name and I am only glad that she didn't call me Anouk.

I live down the street from the drive-in and around the corner from Mom and Dad. I'm closing in on fifty, I have an eleven-year-old son, a very nice ex-husband, and the world as I know it is coming to an end.

I don't know if I can explain this to you, the way I feel about the closing of the Halfmoon. I never worked there—though almost every teenager in Halfmoon Bay did at one time or another. I'm not really a movie buff. I just see whatever—and I mean *whatever*—is on at the drive-in.

But I can count the number of Saturday nights I haven't been at the Halfmoon on my fingers and toes. There were a few weeks of vacation, the night Hayden was born—I followed, of course, in Mom's footprints when I named my child—and the one summer the year I turned thirty, when the drive-in was closed for renovations.

So the Halfmoon Drive-In is closing, and if I had the money to fight the developers for the land, I'd buy it and run it myself. Because I'm not entirely sure what I'm going to do with myself on Saturday nights without it.

Hayden is getting to the age where he'd probably be just as happy to play games on the computer on Saturday night. But me? I remember the years when seven or eight of us would pile into somebody's station wagon to take advantage of the carload discount. I try to forget the years I didn't have dates but went anyway with girlfriends or my parents. I think about the years when Hayden was young enough to sleep in the back while Brad and I watched the double feature, and the few years since Brad left for the mainland. Since then, I've watched Hayden, too, come to love the drive-in. And now all of those years are coming to an end.

I'm simplifying this because I don't want to admit the reality—that the Halfmoon means so much more to me than just someplace to go on a Saturday night.

This sounds stupid coming from a woman who lives in one of the most beautiful places in the world, loves her parents, has a perfect child and a devoted following for the pottery she makes in the studio in her backyard, but the Halfmoon Drive-In feels like home to me.

And I'm not sure what I'll do without it.

CHAPTER 2

On the Waterfront

My mother loves to tell the story of my conception, and you can imagine how much I hated that as a teenager. She generally saves it for anniversaries—of my conception, of her and Dad's wedding, of my birth—so, no matter what, I hear it at least three times a year. She also tells it whenever she's had a couple of glasses of wine, which means she really tells it at every special occasion—from Easter to school plays to Halloween, Thanksgiving and Christmas.

Both Hayden and I have heard it so often we can tell it with Mom's voice, her slight British accent, her extremely ladylike gestures and her dockworker's disregard for the language used in polite company.

She always begins in exactly the same way.

"I don't know," she simpers, waiting for us to enthusiastically respond to her query, "if I've ever told you this story."

We, including whomever happens to be in the room,

jump in with a resounding, *Yes, you've told us before*, but she ignores us.

"It was just after Labor Day and Bill and I had been dating all summer. He was the hottest boy—" my mother watches a lot of television and is even quicker than Hayden at picking up new phrases, the meaning of some of which I don't even want to guess at "—the hottest boy I'd ever seen. Those tight jeans and white T-shirts. Just like Brando."

My dad, who generally tries to halt the story before it begins, always gives in at this point, a reminiscent smile blooming on his face. I wonder if he still sees himself as Brando? If when he looks in the mirror, instead of the slightly stooped, balding man with a face full of sun spots and laugh lines he sees a young, husky, handsome Marlon Brando look-alike?

"Built like a boxer—" Mom smiles "—and he had moves like a dancer. Or an octopus."

Dad grins back at her and lunges. She evades him with a giggle and a look that promises *later*.

Now they're collaborating in the story, and I settle back to hear it one more time.

I swear Mom told me this as a bedtime story before I was capable of remembering it, because it seems to be the first thing I consciously knew—my mother's voice comparing my father to Brando.

In some ways, I agree with her. My dad definitely

deserves an award for the best husband, father and grand-father, the best man I know. But Brando? My dad's short and as thin as a light pole, wiry rather than muscular. He'd play Brando's funny best friend in a movie, the one who makes everyone laugh and tells the girl what a wonderful guy his friend is.

"Bill was away all week during the summer, down in the city loading cargo ships," Mom goes on. "He was making big bucks and saving most of it, except what he spent on me on the weekends. So by the time he finished work and got home, we only saw each other on Saturday nights.

"Up until *the* weekend, we spent those Saturday nights at the Way-Inn, eating burgers and watching everyone in Gibsons watching us. No privacy, no matter how much we wanted it."

Even after all these years it still isn't easy listening to my mother talk about sex, lust, passion. Hayden loves it, though, his eyes shining as he imagines his grandparents young and in love. Too many movies for that boy—he took them in along with his bottle.

"But I had a surprise for this weekend. The Halfmoon Drive-In had opened that very week and that's where we were going. Darkness, privacy. I couldn't wait."

She always stands up at this point in the story and heads over to the nearest window, her back to her audience, her voice pitched low enough that we all stop moving and lean forward to hear her words. I know she's learned this trick from some actress, but it doesn't make it any less effective.

"I'd decided," Mom says, her voice soft and husky, her forehead against the glass, "that Bill was The One."

Just recently she's begun to capitalize those words. She and Hayden are both overly given to dramatics—I think it's why they get along so well.

"And this was the weekend we were going to do it. I'd decided, and Bill would have done it in the Way-Inn if he could've convinced me of it."

She turns to glance at Hayden and winks, miming putting her hands over her ears. He doesn't, of course. He's heard this story so many times he could recite it along with her.

"Make love. Have sex. Do the horizontal mambo."

I'm grateful when she stops there. Occasionally she'll go on for five minutes with synonyms for sex. Sometimes she cuts it short.

"I was the one who'd been putting the brakes on all summer, but once I'd made up my mind, there was no stopping me. Not that Bill tried.

"We parked in the back row, in the darkest corner. That spot was where I became a woman. And where Aimee—" my name is drawn out to three syllables "—was begun."

Hayden gets to ask the question because he's the youngest.

"How do you know that?"

"Because your mother was born nine months to the day after that Saturday night."

The story doesn't ever end. Not really. Depending on the day, the amount of wine consumed, the level of nostalgia and the age of the guests, Mom divulges more or fewer details. If only women are present—her friends or mine, it doesn't matter—she'll tell everything. And I'm not kidding when I say *everything*.

Even now I think all those details are gross. And I know that word is a throwback to my youth, but I can't help it.

I know things, have known them for as long as I can remember, about my father that no daughter should ever know—which makes it even more amazing that I've never fought with my father, gotten angry with him or tried to distance myself from him. He's a great guy and there's absolutely no getting around it.

It did kind of ruin my desire as a teenager for a dramatic life—having the perfect parents, I mean—but I did my very best to get around it.

I dyed my blond hair black, wore thick eyeliner and dark red lipstick. I carried smokes with me and lit them for effect whenever possible. I couldn't smoke them—I'd promised Dad I wouldn't—but I didn't care. It was all about image.

I looked like Sandra Dee, but I wanted to be Katharine Hepburn in *Long Day's Journey Into Night*. Not the morphine addict, though that was tempting, but the darkness and drama of her life was what I wanted.

Even now I occasionally look at my life and wonder how I got here, living the sweet life, full of family and friends and work I love. I feel like an impostor, as if someday I'm going to wake up and find this is all a dream and I'm going to return to my *real* life.

And I can promise you *that* life won't be a Gidget movie.

CHAPTER 3

The Fellowship of the Ring

The headline was in large type on the front page of the *Sunshine Coast News* in April: *Last Season at the Halfmoon.*

Hayden brought the paper to me, his face—his father's face—a mask of sorrow. The Halfmoon is important to him, too. It's where Brad told us he had to leave and where, when he does get back to visit, the three of us go to try to remain a family.

Brad'll roar up on his bike—last year it was a Ducati, the year before a vintage Indian, though most years it has been a Harley—presents in his saddlebags and a smile on his beautiful face.

Brad Mackey, just like my father, is a wonderful man—warm, giving, funny and as sexy as it is possible for a man to be. But he's a wanderer, a man who can't stay in one place. He tried, desperately, once Hayden was born, but in the end, after five years of watching him bang his wings to tatters in the confines of Halfmoon Bay, I had to let him go.

We've managed to stay friends and an odd kind of family for the past six years, mostly—I swear this is true—because of the drive-in. It gave us somewhere to be intimate without being alone. So we didn't have to talk about the oddities of our family, about how much Hayden missed his daddy, and how Brad and I *never* had to talk about whether we missed each other.

I couldn't.

Still can't, for that matter. That's part of the real life I've been ignoring.

When Hayden brought me the newspaper, I glanced at the headline and assumed that it was time again for some upgrades. Past time, by my calculation.

Everything about the Halfmoon had been getting dilapidated. The sound system was still piped in through heavy silver speakers set on poles. The speakers hissed the voices in through your window. And no matter how far you turned the dial, you still had to strain to hear the whispering in the horror films or love scenes.

The screen had been cracked and never properly fixed.

We were watching the second movie of the double feature—*The Two Towers*—for the third time late in September, the last weekend of the summer season. Winter season there was only one film, generally a very bad B movie.

It had rained all day that Saturday, but Brad was in town and Hayden wouldn't think of not going.

"Dad hasn't seen it yet," Hayden said as if it were the saddest thing ever, even sadder than Boromir's death, which made both of us cry every single time it happened, mostly because we knew it was coming. And maybe to Hayden it was just that sad.

Hayden wanted to share everything with Brad, and I wanted him to have what he wanted. So, despite the weather forecast, we packed up the car and went to the Halfmoon.

We piled into my parents' station wagon—which we always borrowed on the Saturday nights they weren't coming with us to the drive-in—with the usual assortment of juice and soft drinks and microwave popcorn already popped. Two kinds—caramel and buttered. Pillows and blankets and chocolates. Cookies, Hayden's favorite sweatshirt, a bottle of Pinot Noir for Brad and me and two glasses. My family takes moviegoing seriously.

The wind had picked up by the time we pulled into our usual spot, right in the middle of row six, a short walk to the washrooms.

The speaker squawked a little and hissed a lot, but we'd tried every single parking spot at the drive-in and this one was the best. The sound quality didn't matter, anyway. Hayden and I knew most of the dialogue by heart, so we didn't care. And Brad would, as always, spend as much time watching Hayden as he would the movie. He didn't care, either.

I'd stopped and filled up with gas on the way over. Once September hit, the nights were cool enough to run the heater at least part of the time, and this night we'd also be running the wipers. Seeing Aragorn through the click-click of the wiper blades was *not* my idea of a good time.

Saruman roared in the tower as the weather roared around us, but we were warm and safe in our metal cocoon.

It was odd, but the cracking of the screen wasn't sudden or loud but subtle, as if a magician had discreetly touched his wand to the top of the screen and drizzled a small drop of some screen-cracking substance onto it and then said, *Go, but slowly.*

A thin line appeared at the top of the screen, black against the white of the wizard's robes and hair.

"Dad, it's the projector again," Hayden said. "I bet they turn it off to fix it."

He settled himself happily back into his nest of blankets and Brad's arm. Anything that extended this outing was okay by Hayden.

We waited for the announcement while the line slowly creeped down the screen and into Saruman's beard. Then we watched it flow down his robe. We waited some more.

The black line lengthened down the screen until it reached the middle and then stopped. A slight distortion appeared in the top half of the picture, a wobble.

A dark figure in a slicker appeared in the rain and wind,

scurrying up the steps to the bottom of the screen. He stopped there for a few minutes, looking like a bug on the cloaks of the hobbits, and then rushed down and away.

"Now," Hayden insisted, satisfaction in his voice, "now they'll stop it."

And they did. For the first time in the history—at least my history—of the Halfmoon Drive-In, they canceled the movie and refunded our money.

Hayden was philosophical and more than willing to spend the first month of school bragging about witnessing the screen ripping apart in the storm. I'm sure his stories were more exaggerated than the actual event—he was eight, after all, and comes from a long line of storytellers.

We took our popcorn and our wine home, plugged *The Fellowship of the Ring* into the DVD player and stayed up late watching the band of friends make their way across Middle Earth.

That winter, Hayden and I watched as one of the fishermen from up the coast sewed up the rip in the screen with tiny invisible stitches using fifty-pound test line. Then, once the worst of the rains were over in the spring, the center of the screen was plastered.

And now, years later, the plaster is cracking like the screen beneath it and foreheads have bumps they were never meant to have and planes have cracks in their fuselages or the sun a black streak right through its heart.

I know there can't be the money—it's only a tiny drive-in with a small clientele—to buy a new screen and a new sound system. I know that the developers who haunt the Sunshine Coast for big plots of land will have offered a sum of money that no one could ignore. But I wish it could be different.

I have, each week since Hayden brought me the paper, taken a hundred dollars from my savings account and bought lottery tickets. I could win, right? And if I did, I'd buy the Halfmoon Drive-In right out from under those developers.

I haven't told anyone about this idea.

In fact, I haven't talked about the drive-in closing. Because I'm sure whoever I talk to about it will think I'm crazy.

I feel crazy. Crazy with loss and sorrow and pain, as if some crucial part of me is being ripped out of my body—my heart or my lungs or my womb.

How can I tell anyone that I feel as if my heart is breaking, that I've lost my home, that I don't know how I'll make it through the rest of my life?

They'll say, "It's only a movie theater," or, "You can go down to Sechelt. They have a whole bunch of screens there," and they'll be right. And it won't change how I feel about it.

So I buy lottery tickets and lie in bed every night making lists in my head of how I'll refurbish the drive-in if I win.

I'll order a new screen and a new sound system. I'll put

up new swings and a jungle gym in the playground. I'll upgrade the concession stand and definitely put hot water in the washrooms.

But I haven't won. Not even a dollar. Not even a free ticket.

The drive-in will not be saved. Not by me, not by anyone. And I'm going to have to figure out how to live with that.

CHAPTER 4

Quest for Fire

I've never spent much time figuring things out. I'm the kind of person things happen to rather than the kind of person who goes out and makes things happen.

Someone—a short-term boyfriend before I met Brad—once told me that I lived that way because my childhood was so happy. If I'd had parents who fought or died or got divorced, he'd said, I'd be more of a go-getter.

Well, he go-getted himself right out of my life, but he might have been right about me.

My best friend—Tabatha Joanne Miller, T.J. for short—is a perfect example of a woman whose life is hell, at least compared to mine.

The two of us gravitated together in first grade because everyone laughed at our names. I guess we figured that if we were friends, there'd be at least one other person in school who wouldn't make fun of us. And we never have, no matter what has happened in our lives—and there have been plenty of things that happened in T.J.'s life that were embarrassing at the very least.

And I have to admit that ever since Mr. Go-Getter said that to me, I've been comparing.

T.J.'s mom left her dad and three kids when T.J. was twelve. T.J.'s been trying to fill her shoes ever since.

She still looks after her dad, watches over her two younger brothers—who, even though they're both around forty, continue to act like teenagers—and worries incessantly about her no-account husband, money and her daughters.

It's amazing we've stayed friends through all of the stuff she's lived through. Her kids are ten and twelve years older than mine—she got married much younger than I did—but I swear T.J.'s girls are still more trouble than Hayden, even though they've long since moved down to the city.

But to get back to the point, I don't know what to do about my feelings because—and I hate to admit this even to myself—I'm not sure I've ever had them before.

Perfect childhood. Check.

Perfect parents. Check.

Perfect husband. Check.

Okay, okay, I know you're laughing about that, seeing as we're divorced, but it's true. Brad—and this is another thing I hate to admit, *especially* to myself—is the love of my life. And I'm pretty sure I'm the love of his.

But he's got an itch that has to be scratched, and I encouraged him to go scratch it. I couldn't bear to see him slide into bored, restless imprisonment. So he travels, writes articles about where he's been for motorcycling magazines, sends three or four letters a week to Hayden and pays for his trips by rebuilding bikes.

Every biker knows who he is. They all call Brad Mackey when they want an Indian or a Ducati or a vintage hog rebuilt. He isn't cheap, but he's damn good.

I could have held him—Hayden would have been a fine set of shackles—but I didn't even try. If it's ever going to work between us, it'll have to be when Brad's ready to settle down in Halfmoon Bay and be happy about it. So I'll rephrase.

Perfect *ex*-husband. Check.

Perfect child. Check.

Perfect job. Check.

Perfect life. Double check.

So why am I obsessing over the drive-in? I don't know and I don't have the insight to figure it out. I feel a bit like that woman in *Quest for Fire*, looking for something she's not even sure exists and doesn't have the tools which will extrapolate that far into the future.

"T.J.?"

She picks up the phone on the first ring, which is a bad sign. It means she's expecting a call from someone—and the only calls she gets on her extraprivate line, except the ones from me, are bad ones.

I get calls from Mom, Dad, Hayden and even Brad to tell me good news. I get calls from the stores that carry my pottery to order more. I even get calls from T.J. to tell me about some big sale she's made.

But T.J. gets totally different kinds of calls. She hears from her brothers, her husband and her daughters—all asking for money. She gets calls reporting that her dad's having a worse day than usual or that her husband—Chris the idiot—has lost his job or totaled his truck. Again.

But T.J., despite the disaster of her life, has a whole bunch of qualities I don't. She handles whatever life throws at her, she fixes things and she makes about five times as much money as I do. She sells vacation condos to seniors. Talk about being in the absolutely right place at the absolutely right time.

T.J. is a go-getter. She goes and gets the sales, the money, the red Porsche Boxster. She goes and gets the new agency and the team of hot young salespeople. And this week she's out getting a piece of land all of her own to develop.

"T.J.?" I say again. "It's me."

"Oh?" she says, sarcasm skimming the surface of her voice like fat on turkey gravy.

"I've been talking to you on the phone for thirty-five years and you have to tell me who you are? Please, Aimee—" she's the only person except Brad who refuses to call me "Amy" "—don't be an idiot. Not today, okay?"

"Sorry," I say, spitting out the word without thought. Once thought kicks in, I try again. "What's wrong?"

"Dad. He gets worse every day."

"Did you see him this morning?"

T.J. stops by the retirement home every morning. I'm convinced the muffin and coffee she shares with her dad is the only meal she eats half the time.

"Hmm," she hums, the pain deepening the sound. "I thought—" she pauses "—you might be his nurse."

"I'll drop by this afternoon."

I know T.J. won't be able to get away, so she needs me to go and make sure he's as okay as possible. T.J. hated putting him in the home, but once he had the stroke, she had no choice.

And I'm happy to go. I like visiting her dad. He never remembers who I am, but the nurses give me coffee and I get to eat half a dozen homemade cookies before I leave.

"Thanks."

T.J. doesn't like anyone—even me—to know she might need help, but we've worked out a system. I pretend to be completely helpless about the financial side of my business—I'm not and she knows it; she was in Senior Bookkeeping with me and I got the highest marks in the class. She helps me with my business plan and taxes and allows me to repay her by helping with her dad.

"How are the girls?" I ask, cringing the moment the

words are out of my mouth. I'm just trying to postpone the real reason I'm calling.

"Don't know. I haven't heard from them this week. Or last week, either."

I think that's a good thing—they only call when there's trouble—though I don't, of course, say so.

"And Chris?"

God, I must be absolutely desperate to avoid asking her to help me figure out what's wrong with me. I *am* absolutely desperate to avoid it.

"He's up the coast fishing for the summer."

I hear the words she doesn't say—*And I wish he'd stay there*—and respond to them. "Do you think he'll stay up there? He likes fishing. At least…" I stop because saying *That's all he's ever done and not very well at that* would be downright rude, even if it is the truth.

She snorts and I know everything is okay between us. That knowledge gives me the courage to ask her.

"Can we have dinner tonight? I need your help."

"It's not tax time. Your work is selling everywhere, even in the city. Hayden's doing well in school. Brad's in Malaysia."

T.J.'s not the only one who knows all of my business, she's just the only one who learns it from me. The Sunshine Coast is a very small place and everyone knows everything. We even have our own gossip queens who, I swear, know even more than everything. So I'm not surprised T.J. knows things I haven't told her. Mostly I'm surprised that she doesn't know why I'm calling.

"So what is it?"

"I need your help to figure out why I'm such a mess about the Halfmoon."

"Huh?"

"The Halfmoon's closing at the end of the summer."

"It always closes for a couple of weeks for cleanup at the end of the summer."

"It's closing forever."

"Oh."

And I hear the wheels turning in her head. One wheel is thinking about me and wondering what the hell is wrong with me—not that she'd say it. At least I don't think she would. The other wheel is wondering about the property.

"It's already sold," I say, telling her what I'd read in the morning's paper. "A mall developer. Upscale."

I didn't know that the developer was upscale, but once you've been reading the *Sunshine Coast News* for more than a couple of years you can read between the lines.

"Oh," she says again and I know I've lost her.

"Dinner," I say, loudly enough to break into her thoughts. "Tonight. Seven o'clock. My place."

I repeat each piece of information slowly and precisely, hang up and then send her an e-mail to confirm. T.J. on the hunt is a one-track creature.

Hayden can stay at Mom and Dad's for the night, and I'll pick him up tomorrow on my way to the drive-in.

Six weeks.

What am I going to do?

CHAPTER 5

The Piano

Friday night does not go at all as I'd planned when I'd phoned T.J. in the afternoon.

T.J. shows up eventually, but she's in worse shape than me. When I hug her I see that her roots are showing—and T.J.'s a fanatic about her hair. Her black panty hose—no one else wears black panty hose on the Sunshine Coast at any time of the year, let alone the summer—have a run from her ankle to her knee, and her turquoise silk blouse has a grease spot right over her left breast.

I hold her tighter and listen to her force herself to breathe.

I haven't seen her like this since her mother left, and though I'm scared to death to ask her, I know what my duty is. Best friends don't hesitate.

"T.J.? Honey?" I pull her with me to the lounge chairs on the back porch and put a glass of sangria in her shaking hand. Looking at her, I wish I'd made something stronger.

Double martinis. Straight tequila. Scotch on the rocks. But the sangria will have to do.

"What is it?" I ask after she's gulped down the first glass and I've poured her another.

She doesn't look at me when I speak. This is a very, very bad sign, because T.J. believes passionately in sales techniques and she never, in her personal or professional life, forgets to make eye contact.

"T.J.? Tell me, okay?"

She shrugs her shoulders and holds out her again-empty glass. Her fire-engine-red polish is chipped. I pour her and myself another drink, then gulp mine down. It's bad, very bad.

I ask one more time, thinking of one of T.J.'s dad's favorite sayings—"Third time's the charm"—and hoping it's true.

Because if T.J. doesn't answer me soon, we're both going to be too drunk to do anything other than get into a crying jag. Or a laughing one. I'm not sure which I'd prefer.

But she does answer this time, and for a moment I wish she hadn't.

"It's my dad," she says, the words barely loud enough for me to hear.

My heart clenches and I say stupidly, "He was fine this afternoon." But he wasn't, not really. He has difficulties with his lolling head and his speech. I was an expert at wiping his chin and helping him get the lukewarm tea or chocolate-chip cookie into his mouth rather than onto the floor.

"They're going to have to transfer him upcoast," T.J. says.

Everything that statement means to T.J. rushes through my head. She will lose the center of her life—those morning visits to her dad. If he's transferred to Powell River, it's a ferry ride and another hour past that—too far to travel every weekend, let alone every morning.

"I didn't think he was worse," I say. "Not very much, anyway."

"I know, but the nurses say it's too hard to care for him. He's not the only one. George Frome and Theresa Romero are going to go, as well."

"But the nurses love your dad."

I don't get it, but of course I do, I'm just trying to ignore what I do know. It's all about money—and T.J.'s dad takes up too much time, too much energy. If it weren't for people like him and George and Theresa, the home could be run without nurses or doctors.

"When?" I ask. It's not the right question, but it's the only one I've got.

"In three months."

"So soon? How do they expect you to make arrangements?"

The answer is that they don't care.

My mind races through the possibilities. Can I take him? For a short time but not for long. At least I'm at home most of the day. T.J. can't take him at all; she's already at her limit if not past it.

"What are you doing tomorrow morning?" Now that's the right question.

"Nothing," T.J. says. "Just the usual."

She can't say it, I think. The center of her life has been ripped away and she'll no longer be able to say to anyone who asks what she's doing the next day, "I'm having breakfast with my dad." That sentence will become, like "I'm skipping class" or "I'm studying," something she once said all the time and now has vanished from her speech.

"We need to go down to Gibsons, to the Way-Inn, and we need to get there before noon."

T.J. perks up a little. "The gossip queens?" she whispers.

"Yep."

They probably already know about T.J.'s dad. In fact, I wouldn't be surprised if they'd anticipated it. When I say they know *more* than everything, I'm not kidding. It's almost as if they anticipate what's going to happen.

The best part is that they're creative. If anyone can come up with a solution to T.J.'s dilemma, it'll be the gossip queens.

That settled, I watch T.J.'s shoulders relax and the

tension lines around her mouth disappear. And I know she's okay when she screams, "Oh, my God, look at this," and then pokes her finger into the hole in her panty hose and rips it from top to bottom.

I can't help myself. I start giggling and then can't stop. T.J., her head held precariously high, lifts her nose even higher and sniffs.

"You—" she points her finger with the chipped polish at me and speaks in that very precise way she has once she's had a couple too many glasses of wine "—are pathetic. Do you have any idea—" she looks down her nose at my bare legs and tatty cutoffs "—how much these cost?" She tugs at the hole some more and then reaches under her black skirt—on the Sunshine Coast in the summer—and pulls the ripped hose off. "Of course you don't. When was the last time you wore anything other than jeans and T-shirts?"

I try to concentrate enough to answer that question, but the truth is that I can't remember.

"I've had too much sangria to remember," I say.

"Right." T.J. grins. "Blame it on the wine."

"My wedding?" I volunteer, trying at least to sound as if I have myself a little bit under control.

"Oh, please. That was almost—no, it was forever ago."

T.J. flings the panty hose at me, and with more luck than skill, I pluck them out of the air. They feel soft and silky in my hands and I sigh.

KATE AUSTIN   37

"Harvey Keitel," I say, running the hose through my hands and knowing—she's my best friend, after all—that T.J. will know exactly what I'm thinking about.

She smiles at me and grabs one foot of the panty hose, her eyes soft.

"How many times have we seen that movie?"

"Dozens," I say. "Maybe more."

The Piano is one of our default movies. You know the one you watch when you can't think of anything else and you don't want to try a new movie in case you don't like it? We watch Harvey Keitel and Holly Hunter and we always watch the piano scene two or three times.

You know the one I mean, where Harvey's on the floor under the piano and he lifts her skirt just enough to see the hole in her stocking?

Nothing happens, not right then, but I don't think I've ever seen anything more erotic than his finger touching her bare skin through that hole in her stocking.

"What's for dinner?"

T.J. breaks into my erotic musing, which is just as well. Sex has been on the back burner for a very long time, and I don't want anything to disturb its peaceful slumber.

But it's too late for that.

After T.J. falls asleep in the spare room, I take my copy of the movie and slide it into the DVD player in my bedroom. Usually it's Hayden and I watching his favorite movies on rainy winter afternoons or when he's home sick from school. Watching Harvey Keitel alone in my bedroom feels more than a little decadent.

But I don't care. This night I go right to the piano scene and I watch it over and over until my body aches with longing and my eyelids swell with the weight of unshed tears.

I imagine myself on that piano bench, my fingers mindlessly playing notes I cannot hear, every iota of my being concentrating on that half inch of skin. I feel his calloused finger tenderly stroking me, his flesh touching mine. I feel the heat of his breath through the stocking and I feel the pounding of his pulse.

This moment is all about restraint—his *and* mine—and I savor it. I lick my lips and imagine the taste of him. I touch the cool keys of the piano and I imagine the warmth of his skin as I touch him. I close my eyes and feel the damp lick of his tongue on my eyelids.

And all the while I feel his finger. I concentrate on it with every part of me—my brain, my heart, the skin on my arms and legs and between them. I concentrate with my taste buds, no longer imagining the salty taste of his skin but knowing it.

I keep my eyes closed to better see him, his eyes that pierce mine with passion, the shoulders and hips moving restlessly beneath his clothes, the lips that part just slightly whenever he's in my presence.

I take a deep breath and smell him, hot and musky and… He smells like no one else in the world.

And I listen carefully, until I swear I can hear the rasp of his finger on my skin.

It's more than I want, more than I can handle, but I can't help myself, no more than the lovers on the screen. We are trapped together in a spiral of longing, of feeling.

It's just half an inch of skin, but he's on me, stroking me, caressing me, loving me.

Sleep eludes me this night—oh, surprise—and so I look like shite—another one of T.J.'s dad's favorite expressions—in the morning. I console myself. T.J. looks much worse.

Her mascara marks her face like a zebra, and the resemblance to that animal is even more striking because her face is as white as those stupid toilet-paper kittens.

Her eyes are lined with red, and she hobbles into the kitchen as if each time her feet touch the ground she wants to scream. If she feels anything like me, she does.

I hand her coffee, black and strong and sweet, and a piece of lightly toasted white bread without butter. She attempts a smile and then tries to stick her whole face into the coffee mug.

"No rush," I say, my voice as low and soft as I can make it and ensure she still hears me. It's still too loud for my ears, but she seems to be okay with it. "We don't need to leave for a couple of hours."

"Good," she mutters into her coffee. "I don't think I could get into a car before that."

I grin, which hurts my head, and then I do it again. There's nothing like an old friend who knows everything about you and still loves you. I touch her shoulder lightly and head up for a shower.

I feel only about one-quarter human when we get in the car. I want to go back to bed, but the thought of Sam's hash browns and an ice-cold Diet Pepsi gives me enough incentive to get in and quietly shut the door behind me.

T.J. slides into the passenger seat, puts her head back and starts snoring.

"Bitch," I whisper, not wanting to wake her. "It's going to be okay. I promise."

CHAPTER 6

Double, double
Toil and trouble

The gossip queens remind me of the witches in *Macbeth*—the old black-and-white Orson Welles version. They're not quite so dark and gloomy, but they do seem to know the future, and I have absolutely no trouble imagining the three of them standing around some cauldron on the beach, waylaying passersby and telling their fortunes.

They speak in riddles, finish one another's sentences, know things they shouldn't, which should make them scary. But they're fun and smart and they hang out at the best restaurant on the peninsula.

They're busy with someone else—I don't know what to call this person: supplicant? customer? client?—when we get there, which suits me just fine. We make eye contact, so they know T.J. and I are here to see them. Then T.J. and I slide into another booth and order breakfast.

By the time they send for T.J.—and not me, and how in the heck did they know it was T.J. and not both of us or just me?—I'm feeling about three-quarters human, a vast improvement, and capable of reading the paper while I wait for T.J.

I watch surreptitiously over the pages shaking in my still shaking hands. I see T.J.'s face go from despair to slightly hopeful. Whatever the three witches have come up with is, at least, a possibility and so it makes me feel better as well.

I smile when T.J. comes back to our booth. The drag in her step is gone, and I know the gossip queens have given her at least some potential solution to her problem.

"A new home is going up just down the street from my office." She flips open her cell phone and punches in a number. "It should be open in six months, and Rose says Dad's a perfect candidate."

I touch her hand, wave for another coffee for T.J. and a Diet Pepsi for me. I settle back and prepare to enjoy myself. Watching T.J. negotiate is a joy. She's an artist, as good at her job as anyone I've ever seen, and I seldom get the chance to watch her in action.

By the time she's finished her coffee, her dad has been promised a spot at the Sunshine Coast Villas, and the old place has guaranteed they'll keep him until the new place is finished.

T.J. slumps back into the red leatherette of the booth and groans.

I hasten to reassure her. "That was amazing. You're a genius, babe, really. No one else could have done it."

"No one else would have been willing to pay what I offered."

"T.J.?"

She knows I worry about her financial risk-taking. It's not for me. Sure, she's done fine so far, but I've watched her in the months when things aren't going so well and she's working herself into the ground.

"I'll figure it out," she says, her voice muffled by the mug she's holding to her face.

She's doing it so I can't see her lips trembling, but I recognize the look. Her eyes are bright not with her usual exuberance but with tears. Her cheeks, even through the carefully applied foundation and blush, are pale. And her nostrils flare, a sure sign that hidden behind the mug her lips are shaking.

"T.J.? What is it?"

I know it's about money, it has to be. Everything else sounds perfect. And I know she's already at the end of her financial rope. Overextended big-time.

The new agency, two kids who always need more money, a husband whose idea of contributing to the family coffers is using his own money—occasionally—to buy gas for the truck that she pays for. Plus she helps out her baby brothers—forty and thirty-eight years old—each time they try to start their own business.

This time, this business, they're doing well. But there's no guarantee. And the others? Her daughters and her husband? They're just a drain on T.J.'s limited resources, though I can't say that out loud.

T.J.'s never once begrudged the time or the money she spends on keeping her family afloat. It's what keeps her going and makes her the person she is, the woman I love like a sister.

Ever since her mom left, T.J.'s been holding things together, keeping everyone happy. I wish she'd spend just a tiny bit of that energy on keeping herself happy, but I don't think it's in her.

"T.J.?"

She puts the mug on the table, and I see that she's somehow managed to adjust her face to reflect the calm, collected saleswoman of the year she believes herself to be. And the offer of help that had been on my lips is quelled by that look.

No one is allowed to offer help to T.J. when she's in saleswoman-of-the-year mode, not even me. I make a mental note to make my own visit to the gossip queens—when T.J.'s not around. They might help me figure out a way to get some money to T.J. without her balking.

Because I have enough of it to give her a little relief.

Work is going better than well. I just got an order for almost four hundred of the cat plates I made for the craft fair last summer. Someone wants to use them for a wedding.

I laughed right out loud when the distributor told me that, but I stopped laughing when I received the deposit check, more money than I normally make in six months.

Not that I'm poor. I own my house thanks to Brad and my parents and my work, have a little money put away for a rainy day, but I don't need much, either. So the deposit money could just as easily go to T.J. She'll pay me back when she can.

I shouldn't have started thinking about the cat plates. I have no idea how I'm going to make them in time for the wedding. I've been having these weird dreams about the plates ever since I got the check in the mail:

I'm in the studio and shards of broken pottery are piled up around me. They are pink and green and black and gold—the colors of the wedding plates. The piles of pieces are everywhere—on the floor, the tables in the center of the room, the shelves which normally contain finished pieces waiting to be packed and sent off to the stores.

There are no finished pieces on the shelves. Not one.

The kiln is cold, its door shut tight, and even in my dream I realize how odd that is.

I pick up a handful of shards and a tube of glue—I

never use glue in the studio; the only glue in the house is in Hayden's craft box. I try to attach the pieces together. I sit down at the big wooden table in the middle of the room and try assembling the shards into a crooked plate.

I locate a part of a cat's head and then pick up another handful of shards. I scramble to pile all the pieces in a huge mound and begin to sort them.

Heads here.

Leaves there.

Tree trunks in another place.

Abstract edge designs.

Pinks in one pile.

Greens in another.

But there are no bodies. I hurry, slicing my fingers and hand on the sharp edges as I try to find a cat body. Just one.

Amazingly the dream doesn't stop there. I finish my sorting and end up with five piles.

All my cats remain without bodies. I clean out the garbage cans. Still no bodies. I sweep under the tables and chairs and equipment—even picking up the eight-thousand-pound kiln and moving it—reaching corners and spaces which I know haven't been brushed by a broom for years.

Still no cat bodies.

I know, I know. This dream is only partly about the

cat plates. But I can't decipher how it relates to the rest of my life.

I'm sure it means something. About T.J., about Brad's summer visit, about the Halfmoon.

You need to see a dream analyst, I think. It's a joke, but as soon as the thought is fully formed, I'm tempted.

But I know what an analyst would say.

"It's an anxiety dream." And that would be right. There's just not anything I can do about it.

Except start making the damn cat plates.

CHAPTER 7

Star Wars

Maybe I accidentally on purpose forgot to tell my mother. Or T.J. I didn't tell Hayden, either, but that was deliberate.

Brad Mackey, the love of my life, ex-husband and father to my son, phoned me last week. But in the midst of the cat plate and T.J. crises, I manage to put the call out of my head. And thank T.J. and the distributor for helping me to do it.

It is the kind of call an ex-wife doesn't know how to feel about, no matter how good of a relationship she may have with her ex.

"Hey, gorgeous, it's me."

The phone had crackled with the thousands of miles that separate us. I'd assumed he was still in Malaysia—and you'd have to work pretty hard to get much farther away from here than there.

I sometimes wonder whether Brad chooses assignments on the other side of the world so he doesn't have to see us more often. But then I see the way his face lights up at the sight of Hayden and I know I'm wrong.

When his blue eyes darken to the color of a summer storm on the ocean, I know he's angry. When he smiles his motorcycle-devil smile, I know he still wants me.

No, Brad chose Malaysia—and Russia and China and Nairobi before it—because it is an adventure. And Brad Mackey is all about adventure.

So why's he coming back to Halfmoon Bay for a whole summer?

I didn't get an answer to that question, not a real one.

"I've got a break. Hayden's out of school. And I miss you?" he'd said.

I'd laughed because I didn't know how else to respond. He might miss me but not enough, not ever enough. And I'm okay with that. I'm not just saying that, either. I really am okay with that. I spent a lot of time working through this before he left for the first time and I understand him.

The sad thing is that I understand Brad better than I understand myself. I know. Because if I could figure out me, I wouldn't be obsessing about the closing of the stupid drive-in and why I'm so worried, upset and anxious about it. I'd know why I'm so worried, upset and anxious about it.

Nonetheless, having Brad miss me but not quite enough boosts my image of myself as film noir rather than Gidget. All those women have deep, dark secrets. And I have one, too: an unbearable longing for the man who broke my heart, the man I still love.

Still, I'm the only person in the world who knows that secret, and it'll stay that way. Not even T.J. knows—and she's the one person who hears all my secrets, just as I hear hers.

Remembering the phone call, I know I'm going to have to tell everyone about Brad. Mom, Dad, T.J. Especially Hayden. Though I think I might wait on telling him.

Hayden is going through the "terrible twos" almost nine years late. It feels as though he speaks only one word—*no*—and it's always spoken at the top of his substantial lungs.

In one night he turned from an angel child to the dark side—no passing go, no collecting two hundred dollars. I have considered banning Darth Vader—young, old, in training, in any other form—from the house, but I'm not sure I'd survive the battle.

Hayden's always been strong-willed; people tell me only children often are. And that's probably even more true of single male children of single mothers. I don't know about other kids, but I promise you that one day with my son could convince you of that argument.

Even as a baby he knew exactly what he wanted and exactly how to get it. And, unlike now when *no* is his only tactic, he had and he used all sorts of ploys to get his way.

Over the years Hayden has been a master of the sullen silence, the wistful sigh and the martyred smile. He can plead like a telemarketer, argue like a political candidate, guilt me out like a judge.

And he used all these tricks interchangeably so I had no idea of what to expect next. Looking back, I realize Hayden was too slick for me—for anyone, really. Because even though he always got what he wanted, everyone still loved him, even the people he tricked to get his own way.

So I have expectations of my son, of the ways he'll try to get what he wants, and none of what I anticipate from him is being fulfilled this summer.

Add his father into this already volatile situation and who knows what will happen.

I don't. And that scares me.

There are already enough complications in my life. I wanted to say, *Not a good idea right now* to Brad, but I knew I couldn't.

Brad may be an ex, but he knows me almost as well as T.J. does. If I'd revealed my reservations, he'd have known something was wrong and insisted on coming anyway.

Same result, different visit.

Knowing something was wrong, Brad would arrive on his bike like a knight on a white charger and have to solve all my problems—something else he and T.J. have in common. And I'd be unable to resist the steamroller that is this Mackey male when he's concentrating.

Nope. Very bad idea.

So I'd said, "Great. Hayden'll be happy and so will I. I've got a huge order to get out and barely enough time. If I don't have to worry about Hayden, it'll make my life much easier."

I'd considered not telling Brad about Hayden. I really did, but in the end I knew it wouldn't be fair.

"Hayden's going through a spell," I'd said.

"A spell?" Brad had laughed.

He's got the kind of laugh—another thing Hayden inherited—that's contagious. When Brad laughs, his face opens up and glows like a sunflower in the rays of the summer sun. His eyes close, his shoulders shake, his whole body participates.

"A spell," I'd repeated, pulling myself away from the hypnotic effect of Brad's laughter. "I think he's forgotten every word in the dictionary except *no*. And he's forgotten how to brush his teeth or how to shower. It's like living with a two-year-old."

Brad had laughed again.

"I'm glad you're coming," I'd told him truthfully. "I could use a break, and maybe you can snap Hayden out of it. I can't."

"I'll be there in a week, maybe ten days," he'd said and then I almost missed the hesitation.

I knew what he wanted to ask and I'd been wondering what I'd say when he asked it. I still wasn't sure I was doing the right thing for me, but the conversation convinced me that it was the right thing for Hayden, so I'd said it before he'd asked. "Why don't you stay with us? It'll be easier and Hayden will love it."

I think back on that phone call now and wonder how much of my anxiety dream is about having Brad Mackey in my house for most of a summer.

Most of it, I think. Which means that I do know why I'm feeling the way I'm feeling.

Except I don't. Because I've been feeling this way since April and I only found out about Brad two days ago. Damn. Damn. Damn.

I still have absolutely no idea about what's going on with me and I don't know how to find out.

CHAPTER 8

Risky Business

I'm supposed to be thinking about the damn cat plates, but my brain is being overwhelmed by other seemingly more important thoughts.

My mind—and I hate this—keeps spiraling back to Brad's laugh. *Down*, I tell it. *Down*. I don't want to be thinking about him, not in *that* way, not when he's going to be spending weeks under my roof.

I replace thoughts of Brad with thoughts of Hayden, not a better alternative exactly but definitely less risky.

"He'll grow out of it," Mom had said when I'd told her about the phase he's going through, and T.J. had echoed her words. But I wonder how either of them knows because they both brought up girls.

Okay, T.J. sort of brought up her brothers, but I'm not counting them. My mind is my mind and it can work on whatever logic works for it. So there.

Hayden will grow out of it. I just have to figure out a

way to stop myself from strangling him while he does. I consider earplugs—at least I won't have to listen to *no* all the time. The trouble is that the *no* is pretty clear even without the aural clues.

Hayden's face and body radiate *no*. His eyes flame with rejection, his shoulders square up and tense. He keeps his arms crossed over his chest and, whenever possible, he turns his back to me.

His ever-so-eloquent back. Who knew a featureless, T-shirted slab of flesh and bone could speak so clearly?

I could spit, but it won't help.

So I shift my thoughts from Hayden back to the damn cat plates. I can't think of them without the sobriquet—they're ruining my summer.

And that leads me back to the Halfmoon.

It's Saturday and I have to pick up Hayden in an hour. Neither Mom nor Dad has called to complain about their grandchild, so I'm assuming that he's his usual cheerful, sweet self when he's with them. I could spit about that, as well, but it won't help, either.

I've got a calendar above my desk, and all of the remaining Saturdays are circled in red. Thick, deep, bright red—the color, I think, of my heart's blood.

I realize, even as I'm thinking those words, that my reaction to the closing of the Halfmoon is a little over-the-top. Maybe slightly melodramatic. And I want it to be.

I want to be Bette Davis in *Dark Victory* or Gloria Swanson in *Sunset Boulevard*. Those are the women I want to be.

Maybe I'm tired of my Gidget life. Maybe all this angst over the Halfmoon is about change—for me.

My mind, wilful as ever, won't let me linger on that enticing thought but instead goes back to the blood-circled Saturdays.

So I pick up the phone and wait until T.J. answers.

"What do you do with your Saturday nights?" I blurt it out, no hello or how are you, just the question.

"Aimee? Are you okay?"

"Just tell me. What do you do with your Saturday nights?"

I hear her settle back into her chair. I don't have to see her to know that she has a coffee on her desk or that the lines around her mouth become more pronounced while she's considering the answer.

"Depends," she says through a mouthful of coffee. "Sometimes I have dinner with Chris. Sometimes the girls are home and we go down to the Way-Inn."

I nod even though she can't see me, either, and wait for the rest of the answer.

"The best Saturdays—" she sighs and has another sip of coffee "—are when I'm home alone. I take a bottle of wine and some candles up to the bathroom, pour myself a glass and a tub full of sweet-smelling bubbles and I spend the evening there, in the candlelight."

Her chair shifts. She's toeing off her shoes and tucking her feet up under her. T.J. never sits still for long, but when she settles for even a few minutes, her feet are off the ground.

"No music, no light except the candles. No kids, no husband, no one bugging me. I even turn off the ringer on the phone. It's heaven."

"I go to the Halfmoon," I say. "I've been going to the Halfmoon every Saturday night for my entire life."

"What are you going to do come September?" T.J.'s voice is gentle. She may think I'm being an idiot about this, but she's still sympathetic.

"I have absolutely no idea."

And it's the truth.

"Thanks, T.J. I have to go and work on the damn cat plates. And then I'm going to buy some bubble bath."

She laughs, which is what I'd intended, and hangs up.

I'm not laughing.

Because I can't imagine myself into a time past Labor Day. I can't imagine a Saturday night without the Halfmoon. I can't imagine Aimee Anouk King in a life that's different from the one I have now.

The chair slams into my butt almost before I realize I've fallen into it, my legs no longer able to support me.

"Ouch." I try to shuffle myself more comfortably into

the kitchen chair, but its minimal padding isn't really helping. Nor are my evasion tactics.

I've just had an epiphany, but I'm trying desperately to ignore it. And now, when I want my mind to skip from thought to thought, it—with a will of its own—is stuck on the revelation I want to ignore, the epiphany that I'm just certain is going to change everything.

So I head for the studio because there I can focus on some solid thing. Not the damn cat plates—they're too aggravating—but maybe something else.

I sketched a new idea for a mug the other day. Maybe I'll see if I can make it look as good in three dimensions as it does on the page.

But when I look at the sketch again, even it doesn't look right. I play with it a bit, changing the shape, altering the proportions. And now it looks worse.

I change the colors, turning the turquoise into aqua, the beige into a light taupe.

It still looks wrong.

So I try going back to the original, but I can't get back to the design I thought only yesterday was the best thing I'd done in months.

The whole time I work on the sketch, I have to force myself to ignore the epiphany, the revelation. But it's there in the back of my mind, just waiting to leap to the front the moment I stop consciously ignoring it.

I try a couple more revisions to the design, but now nothing looks good. I know I'm wasting time so I shut up and lock the studio.

I check the drive-in bag—yes, the Halfmoon has its own special bag that we use only for Saturday nights—to make sure it's packed. I get in the car and head over to pick up Hayden, Mom and Dad. It doesn't matter what movie is playing—never has, never will—we're just doing what we've always done.

And I spend the five-minute trip in conversation through the rearview mirror with my unruly mind.

It's an epiphany. You can't ignore epiphanies.

"I'm not ignoring it, I'm postponing it, all right?"

I don't think you can do that.

"Can so."

Cannot.

"Can so."

All I can say is that it better be a really good movie or you'll be dealing with it in this small car with the whole family watching you.

My mind croons to itself for a while, humming *I can't get no satisfaction.*

You sure you don't want to stop the car and deal with this now? It would be better if you did. Really.

"No. Not now. Later, when I'm home and Hayden's asleep and I have time. Lots and lots and lots of time."

I don't say any of this out loud. I guess I don't have to because I am having this discussion with myself, after all, but I also need to have a couple of glasses of wine before I deal with this.

Okay, my mind says with a sigh, *but I guarantee you won't enjoy the movie.*

Will so.

I'm glad I didn't have a sibling, because I'm not sure I could have stood to have this kind of conversation every single day. It's bad enough having it with Hayden.

I take my eyes off the rearview mirror and smile. I'm here at my parents' house and the three of them—Mom and Dad and Hayden—will distract me until we get to the Halfmoon.

And once we get there and get settled the three of them will take my mind off everything else. They'll talk through the movie, they'll ask me to pass them bottles or napkins or snacks. They'll discuss the trailers and the movies, and even when there's an important scene, they'll talk right through it. I don't know how they ever remember any movie.

That's always been the way of it.

Labor Day is coming.

CHAPTER 9

Gone with the Wind

You want to know about the epiphany that keeps me up all Saturday night? And will keep me up all night for weeks to come?

I'm not sure yet that I know what it means even after eight solid hours of contemplation. But I'll tell you what I do know.

I know that my failure of imagination—that I was and still am unable to imagine myself in another life—is the reason I am where I am.

Here in Halfmoon Bay and not traveling the world with Brad, not trying something else on a Saturday night, not even taking vacations.

I am living a life even more appalling than the Gidget life I despise. I am living a life filled with, completed by, fulfilled in routine. And what the hell kind of life is that?

My life is all about comfort. It's about doing the same thing, the same way, at the same time, over and over again.

Of course I couldn't leave to travel with Brad. Of course

I couldn't move to the city to go to college. Of course I couldn't join T.J. in her new business.

I had a life where I was comfortable. And safe. And never once challenged to rise out of it.

Well, this summer is managing to challenge all of those things I've been taking for granted.

Can I cope?

I'm not sure.

And I'm not sure I even want to think about it. The one thing I do know is that events are conspiring against me.

Brad.

T.J.

Hayden.

The damn cat plates.

And now my father.

Last night he didn't go to the Halfmoon with us. Not a unique event but definitely unusual.

What was unique was the reason he gave for staying home alone.

"I want to work on the computer," he'd said. This from a man who avoids any and all electrical appliances and electronics. I mean, he still has a push mower.

Hayden programs my parents' DVD player, changes the settings on the stove, the security system, the bedroom clock radio. Dad doesn't get LCD readouts, let alone logging on to the computer.

Yet there he'd stood, his face as stubborn as I'd ever seen it, insisting that he wanted to stay home with the computer.

So we went without him, and the movie—*Superman Returns*—and the worry about my father were more than engaging enough for me to avoid more than a few scattered moments of distraction about the epiphany.

Of course, that means my mind had plenty of time to think about things while I was gone. The minute I turn off the light, it starts as if it had never stopped.

This is important, it says, as if I didn't already know, as if it isn't clear that the reason I'm avoiding this discussion is that I'm scared to death at how important this is.

"I know it is. And I admit what I've known since the very moment of having the epiphany. It's going to change my life, isn't it?"

I hope so, because this one is dead boring.

"It is, but it's comfortable, and I'm comfortable in it."

You're in a rut. Always have been.

"And what's wrong with that? It's a pretty good rut, a penthouse-and-champagne kind of rut."

Doesn't matter how dressed up it is, doesn't matter how expensive the wine, a rut is a rut.

"But…"

There are no buts. Everything I've said to myself is true, every argument has been countered—by me, by the other me—and there's not much use in continuing to fight with myself.

I sigh and roll over, trying to hammer my pillow into submission. It doesn't submit, so I try to settle into its lumpiness.

I'll deal with all this stuff tomorrow. Or the next day. Or, more accurately, after Brad's gone and the damn cat plates are finished and shipped.

THE NEXT MORNING IS a brilliant, sunny day with enough breeze to keep the temperature perfect. I should be delighted, but I'm not. The perfect day just makes me realize how unsettled I am.

Hayden makes it worse.

And then my father makes it even more worse.

I wander past Hayden's den—it would be unfair to rooms to call it a room—around ten. Silence. And then again around eleven. It's still dark and a miasma of "Don't come in" surrounds the door. If I believed in magic, if I thought Hayden might be interested in anything beyond bits and bytes and RAM and ROM, I would suspect him of putting a keep-out spell on the door.

But it's simply a manifestation of his *no* self, the new and unhappy boy who has recently replaced my lovely child. The evil twin is now in the ascendant, and there's little I can do about it except continue to stop myself from strangling him.

When I pause outside his door, I find myself wishing that he'll stay asleep so I don't have to deal with him, not today, not this morning, but it isn't long before the monster appears from his den.

His hair stands up in greasy spikes from his head. The evil twin is not fond of showers and will only be forced into the water every four or five days. I hope today will be one of them.

He's wearing an orange T-shirt that Brad brought from South Africa four or five years ago, which should tell you just what kind of shape it's in. It's too small, but it's Hayden's favorite. He wears it every day that it's not in the laundry and more than a few days when it should be. His bare feet are dirty and his shorts are too big.

He doesn't speak when he sits down opposite me at the table, his eyes still marked with sleep.

"Hey, hon," I say, keeping my voice cheerful. "What do you want for breakfast?" I glance at the clock and add, "Or lunch?"

"Dunno," he mutters, the second most-used word in his recent vocabulary.

"Toast? Eggs? Pancakes?"

He doesn't have to say it. His face screams *no*.

"Not breakfast, then." I turn away to compose myself and remind the angry part of me of the sweet boy he was only a month ago. And will be again—sooner rather than later if I'm very, very lucky.

"How about tuna salad?" The *no* expression on his cranky face intensifies. "Grilled cheese?" A slight lightening of the *no* and I take that for a yes.

Much of my conversation with Hayden over the past month has been a series of guesses, mostly wrong, on my part. The noes have been crystal clear, but the yeses are much harder to decipher. It's as if he is refusing to speak such a positive word or, indeed, to exhibit any positive emotion at all.

When I phone T.J., she says it's just a phase.

"Both my girls went through it," she says. "You're lucky. I hear that when boys do it, it generally doesn't last long. With both Eve and Alice it was years." She sighs, a sure sign of distress. "Those five or six years were the longest and hardest of my life. I wouldn't wish them on anyone. But they did finally get over it."

Yeah, I think, *when they moved out of Halfmoon Bay and you only had to see them once a month or so.* I keep those thoughts to myself.

"Thanks," I say. "That's reassuring. Only five more years to go?"

"I'll keep my fingers crossed for you," she says, "but I don't promise anything except aggravation."

"Thanks again."

The trouble is that she's often right about kids. I've counted on her to get me through sleepless nights, teething, toilet training, the trauma of kindergarten and learning to ride a bike. She's guided me through birthday parties and nightmares and clinging.

All I can do is hope that she's wrong about this *no* thing. I've got my fingers crossed, as well.

The grilled cheese has disappeared from the plate in what seems like one bite, and Hayden vanishes almost as quickly. I'm tempted to call him, to insist he clean his room, take a shower, mow the lawn, but I can't bear the thought of the battle.

At least I know where he is, safe at the computer playing some sort of world-building game. When he used to allow me in his room, I occasionally watched him play and marveled at the complex web of cities, countries and civilizations the players managed to grow on the screen. Now, of course, I only know he's playing the same game because I hear the opening music when he logs on.

And that opening music reminds me of Dad and his computer excuse from last night.

Dealing with Dad has got to be easier than dealing with Hayden. So I go with it and start exploring the possibilities.

He can't be using the computer; I'm not sure he even knows how to turn it on. It must have been an excuse. But for what? Is he ill?

"Hayden, I'm going over to Grandma and Grandpa's. You want to come with me?"

There's a slight hesitation—which I take as a good sign—before the inevitable no floats down the stairs.

"I'll be back in a couple of hours." I hesitate, as well, and then think, *What the hell*. "Have a shower while I'm gone. And get your laundry together. I'll do it this afternoon."

I'll still have to drag the orange T-shirt from his back, but I might as well try for a running start. Another, far more emphatic no slams down the stairs. This one I ignore.

"Two hours, Hayden. Shower and laundry. You can accomplish that in fifteen minutes."

I grab my wallet and head out. The walk, though short, will do me good, maybe even dispel some of my anger.

Actually, just being away from the insistent pull of Hayden's no makes me feel better. I forget how wearing it is because I'm used to it. Maybe Brad being here will help. He'll take Hayden camping or fishing, and I'll get some time to myself to work on the damn cat plates.

The walk doesn't help much, but at least I'm out of the house, away from Hayden, the plates, the sameness of my life. Not that my parents' life is any different.

Dad's mowing the lawn when I arrive. Of course he is. It's Sunday, it's the summer, it's two o'clock. My dad has a routine that's as tightly scheduled and adhered to as reveille on an army base.

He doesn't need it written down anywhere—though he does—it's so much a part of him. And Mom. And me and

Hayden. It's a different schedule since he's retired, but it's equally stringent.

That's the reason I'm worried about him. Saturday nights are Halfmoon Drive-In nights, have been for forty-five years. I think he's missed even fewer of those Saturday nights than I have over the years, and for him to miss one to work on the computer is so unusual as to be more than disturbing. It's frightening.

I smile and kiss his cheek as I pass by on my way into the house. I want to talk to Mom first, so two o'clock is the perfect time to arrive. It takes Dad exactly forty-five minutes to mow the lawn. He could do it in fifteen with a gas or electric mower, but he swears he likes the sound of the blades.

As soon as he's finished mowing, he'll take another fifteen minutes to clean the mower and another thirty to sharpen the blades. He's owned this mower ever since he and Mom bought this house almost thirty years ago, and it looks as if it's brand-new. The blades shine. The handle gets painted at the beginning of each summer, the blades oiled every month even in the winter.

Dad has an account book—not for accounts but for his schedule. It has columns for each year for the past thirty, and each item is checked off as he does it.

Put away lawn mower. October 15.

Put up Christmas lights. November 11.

Take down Christmas lights. January 6.

Fertilize the front lawn. April 12.

Fertilize the back lawn. April 13.

You get the picture. The book is almost fifty pages long and contains big items like *Paint the house* and tiny items like *Tighten the screws in the light sockets in the kitchen*, each with dates and room for check marks.

My mom's schedule is much more flexible than his. In fact, I'm not sure she has one except for Saturday nights. You know how some retired couples become more and more like each other? Until they even start to dress alike, maybe even look alike?

The opposite's true for my parents. My father has his schedule; my mother doesn't. She does whatever appeals to her—eats, cooks, paints, goes to the Way-Inn for a gossip, walks on the beach—whenever it appeals to her.

There is no set time for meals in my mother's house, which drives my father crazy. It interferes with his routine. When he complains about it, Mom says, "So you cook, then," and he does for a few days until he gets tired of scrambled eggs, sliced tomatoes and burned toast.

"Mom? Where are you?"

"Kitchen," she yells.

I know better than to expect her to be cooking. The kitchen has become so much more than a place to make or eat meals. It's her office, studio, workshop, communi-

KATE AUSTIN   71

cations center—and I'm as likely to find paints, piles of correspondence or balls of brightly colored yarn on the old oak table as I am a pie or a tray of cookies.

Today, though, there's just my mother, a cup of tea steaming in front of her strangely unoccupied hands. My mother is a putterer and she's rarely without something to do.

"Tea?" she asks me quietly.

I nod yes and she pulls a mug from the cupboard to pour me a cup.

"Mom? What's wrong?"

Her smile, normally glowing, has been dimmed like the sun hiding behind clouds.

"I don't know," she says, her hands wrapped around the steaming cup. "It's your father."

"He didn't come with us last night, but that's happened before." I'm trying, desperately, to assuage my mother's fear and deny my own.

It isn't working.

CHAPTER 10

Six Degrees of Separation

The conversation I have with Mom is even less reassuring than the earlier one with T.J. Perhaps it's because it's my dad, but both of us have trouble believing he'll grow out of it. Whatever *it* is.

"It's not just the Halfmoon," Mom says over the click-click of the lawn mower blades. "It's every unscheduled minute. And even some of the previously scheduled ones."

"He spends them in the basement?"

"On the computer."

This doesn't sound at all like my dad. He's an outdoor guy. He worked on the docks his whole life, and any extra time was spent in the garden. Or fishing. Or hunting for wild mushrooms or fiddleheads.

I have trouble imagining—yes, I know, it's a serious flaw—my father in the dark basement. Especially in the summer.

"What's he doing on the computer?"

I think of Hayden and his world-building game and try

to imagine my father doing that or something else as innocuous, but I can't.

Dad loves games, but it's because they're social. We played games when I was a kid and we do the same with Hayden. Cards, Monopoly, Clue, even Twister. And Dad loves them all. The *only* time—and I'm not kidding when I say *only*—I can picture Dad doing something by himself is mowing the lawn, and even then he'll call me or Mom or Hayden every five minutes to ask some question or check something that doesn't need to be checked.

"Does the mower sound rough to you?"

"Is it too early to do this? I'm the only one out here."

"Can you pour me some lemonade?"

Even, when he couldn't think of anything else, "How's school (or work or T.J.'s kids)?"

It extends the mowing process from half an hour to twice that, but he doesn't care. He just schedules it in.

My father hates to be alone. There's no question about it.

"He's in chat rooms," Mom says. "Talking to…well, I don't know exactly whom because he won't tell me. All he says is that it doesn't matter, it's just interesting, not important."

And I can't help but think of all the *interesting* chat rooms I've surfed by in the middle of the night when I couldn't sleep. I school my face into calmness and don't say what I'm thinking, which is, *Oh, my God, my dad is a lurker.*

"Interesting?" I ask, trying not to let my concern—actually, my horror—show in my voice.

"I don't know what he means by that," Mom says, "but it's probably just other guys talking about guy things." She waves her hand around to include the guy things in her house. "You know, fishing and boating and sports. Hockey and football, probably. Maybe a little bit of the Tour de France."

I agree, but I want to rush home and ask Hayden how I can follow in my father's computer footsteps to find out where he's been. And with whom.

And I wonder, too, whether it's something in the water or the pesticides in the tomatoes or some other type of supplement that's affecting only the half of my family burdened with testosterone. Because it looks as if the evil-twin syndrome is also appearing in my father. I wonder if Hayden has infected him.

"I wouldn't worry," I say to Mom and think, *I'm doing more than enough for both of us.* "It's a phase. I went through it, too. When I got comfortable enough on the computer to see what was possible, I spent hours going from one Web site to another. Stayed up all night a couple of times. And then I got over it."

All of which is true, but I don't think this is what's happening to Dad. I don't know why, but his refusal to go to the Halfmoon last night triggered a panic response in me.

I'm going to have to talk to him. But not yet, not until I have more evidence—which I'll have to get without worrying my mom more than she already is. I can't ask Hayden for all sorts of reasons.

Mostly I don't want him to know that we're worried about his grandpa. My dad is one of the two most important men in Hayden's life and the only one on-site most of the time. I don't want—especially during this terrible-two phase—for anything to upset either of them.

Brad will know what to do, I think. And for the first time since the phone call I'm no longer ambivalent about his arrival. Although I'm not happy to have now discovered two reasons to be happy about Brad's visit.

I settle to the more immediate task of cheering up my mother. I coerce her—it isn't difficult—to join me in a little research. Of the shopping kind.

"I've lost it," I say to her as we prowl the streets of Gibsons. "I've committed to these damn cat plates and I can't seem to get at it. And nothing else is right."

"So," she says, taking my arm and leading me into the nearest store, "you need inspiration."

"I guess so," I say, uncertain if that's true. I think what I need is distraction.

I get it in spades. Gibsons is full of craft shops, which are full of the most amazing pottery—some of which is even mine.

The trouble is that I look at it—my pottery, I mean—and feel no connection to it at all. Intellectually I know I created it; emotionally I can't figure out how.

And I suspect that disconnect between heart and brain relates to or is the cause of—damn, another epiphany—all the things that are driving me wild this summer.

For my mother's sake, I pretend to enjoy the shopping, though in the end neither of us buys anything. But I do stroke the pottery of my friends and rivals. I do check out what's selling and what's not. I chat with storekeepers and fans of my work.

Rowena Dale, who I'm sure should be in the Guinness Book of World Records for the most consecutive unconsummated engagements, is buying one of my black-and-rose platters.

"Amy." She makes no pretense toward the French pronunciation of my name. "This is lovely." She lowers her voice. "I'm going to give it as a wedding gift. Do you think you could make me a bowl to go with it?"

I know better than to ask Rowena about the wedding. She's been engaged twenty-seven times at last count—and those are only the ones she talks about—and nary a wedding in sight. It's a sore spot. So I simply answer her question.

I'm happy that I already have one in the studio, because I'm beginning to fear that I might have lost my skill with clay and will have to find a new way to make a living.

Shaking off the worry, I promise to deliver it in a couple of days and move on to the next store.

"She's an amazing woman," Mom says once we're out of earshot, which means at least two stores away. Rowena may be eighty, but she has the hearing of a twenty-year-old. "She looks like she's sixty," Mom continues, "but it's not even that. She still believes that she can find the right man and she keeps on trying. Can't be easy."

After twenty-seven engagements? *Easy* ain't the word.

I agree and try not to think about the courage it takes to keep coming back for that kind of punishment year after year, decade after decade. Rowena Dale's bravery astonishes me.

We're nearing the end of the shops and I'm starting to falter. Keeping up a facade of interested cheeriness in front of my mother isn't easy, especially not with all I've got on my mind.

"Come on," she says. "Let's go to the Way-Inn for a burger and a beer."

"Dad?"

"He'll be fine."

I'm taking Mom out to cheer her up, to help her forget Dad's weirdness, and here she is, as always, taking care of me.

I have to do something about Hayden, but Mom beats me to it, whipping her cell phone from her pocket.

"Bill? Aimee and I are going to have dinner at the Way-

Inn. Run over and pick up Hayden and take him somewhere for something to eat."

She pauses and I know Dad is asking where and what and how long. She cuts off his questions.

"I don't care." A quick glance at me and I shrug. "And neither does Aimee. Pizza, burgers, ice cream cones, whatever. Just get him out of the house and get some food into him. We'll see you later."

I notice she doesn't say when, which means she has more planned than simply a burger and a beer at the Way-Inn. She proves me right by dialing another number.

"T.J.?"

And then another.

"Rowena?"

My mother is all about spontaneity, and by the time she's gone through all the names in her address book there are ten of us meeting for dinner, mostly her friends.

Mom's friends—she has dozens of them—are diverse: doctors, stay-at-home wives and mothers, young and old, rich and poor. My mother gathers women to her as if she were a chocolate shop. And they love her. And because of her they also love and support me. And Hayden. And T.J.

Every one of the dozens of women in my mother's voluminous address book owns my pottery. They give it as gifts on every occasion—which means that everyone on the Sunshine Coast owns it, plus, I swear, at least one person in every single town in Canada.

Because you know that whole six-degrees-of-separation thing? Where you can connect to anyone in the world through no more than six people—as long as you pick the *right* people?

In Canada, if it takes you more than two, you're either an orphan and have lived your entire life in complete isolation or you've just moved here from some country which has never—and I mean *never*—sent a single other immigrant here.

So Mom's friends have sent my pottery far and wide for weddings, birthdays, anniversaries, bar and bat mitzvahs and every holiday known or made up by women. My mark—a dragonfly—is seen by thousands and my Web site gets hits every day from people wanting to add to their collection.

My work is practical use-every-day kind of stuff. Plates, mugs, bowls. It's whimsical and often fun. The way the damn cat plates are supposed to be.

If I could ever finish them. No, let me rephrase that. If I could ever *start* them.

THE WAY-INN IS FLOWING over with laughter when we open the door. Everyone has managed to arrive before us—which is weird as we were only a few minutes away when Mom started calling. But Mom's friends, new or old, all seem to be on the same wavelength. I'm willing to bet that at least half of them were in their cars and on their way into Gibsons—without knowing exactly why—when she spoke to them.

I sit down somewhere in the middle of the crowd and relax right into the chaos. This scene—many women around a table—is a constant for me. I've been sitting surrounded by high-pitched voices making music for as long as I can remember.

There is something about the voices of a group of women that calms me, comforts me, occasionally excites me. And my mother, as she always has, knew exactly what I needed on this particular evening.

I am happy when Mom and T.J. take over the ordering of the wine, when T.J. heads over to the jukebox and loads it up with songs we've been singing and dancing to for years, songs that get our hearts pounding, our feet tapping and voices singing.

I am even happier when Sam comes out of the kitchen to help us clear off the makeshift dance floor and leads Rose right into a foxtrot.

This night is exactly what I need and I don't even have to ask for it. That's family. That's friends.

CHAPTER 11

Pinocchio

I felt much better—more in control, more confident, almost ready to start on the damn cat plates—when I arrived home last night, but I crashed right back into messy Aimee during the subsequent hours of tossing and turning alone in the dark.

My midnight fretting is rarely productive. Last night, though, was more useful than usual. I have a plan—not for the damn cat plates—but for Hayden, who is slightly less sullen when Dad drops him off at home the morning following the night at the Way-Inn (okay, almost afternoon).

Mom had driven me home the night before, and one of her friends had done the same for T.J.

"You're too tired to drive," she'd said, her euphemism for *You've had one glass of wine too many.*

She also had two other women follow us home in our cars so we'd have them in the morning. Despite her conversion to complete spontaneity in her own life, my mother might as well be a general. Planning, arranging, organizing—those things make up a big part of my mother's natural skill set.

I had decided during my sleepless night—a little too much wine always has that effect on me—to tell Hayden and the rest of the clan about Brad's summer plans.

I start slow.

"Did you have breakfast with Grandma and Grandpa?"

He nods and heads for the stairs, but I stop him.

"I need to talk to you," I say, immediately dispelling any possible positive slant to this conversation.

Hayden shrugs. I've learned to interpret his responses from his back as it's pretty much all of him I've seen for weeks. This shrug, higher with the right shoulder than the left and including a tilt of his head to match, means, *I'll listen, but it better be good or I'm outta here.*

"It's about your dad."

Wrong again. The shoulders collapse into his shoulder blades, and though I can't see his face, I know there are tears in his eyes.

I'm an idiot this morning because now he expects bad news. Duh. All those hours of darkness scripting this conversation haven't helped a bit.

I rush in, forgetting the script, wanting only to make my boy feel better.

"He'll be home in a week or ten days."

I hear, only because I'm listening for it, the tiniest of sniffs and see a slight relaxing of his hands.

"He's going to stay for the rest of the summer," I say and am rewarded by seeing his face when he turns, wearing not quite a smile but a definite lightening of the gloom.

"Is he going to stay with us?"

"I asked him to," I say. "And I'm pretty sure he wants to." I think for a minute, trying to avoid another misstep, then add, "Is that okay with you?"

"I guess so," he says, but I ignore the unenthusiastic words and use his face to gauge his response.

He's not smiling. The evil-twin mask pretty much precludes a smile, and laughs are out of the question. But Hayden, for the first time in weeks, looks as if he might consider the world to be an okay place. He's not convinced, the expression says, but he's willing to give it one more chance. This time, though, the world better not screw it up.

I hope so, too. Not just for Hayden's sake but for mine and Brad's. The balance of our lives is always more precarious when Brad's around, none of us quite certain how to act.

It's as if we're all walking on a frozen lake in late spring. It looks solid, all the signs say it is solid, but you have to wonder. So we move around each other with more than a touch of caution, listening for the ice to start cracking at our feet.

It hasn't yet cracked, but we've not spent more than a week together at a time in the past six years, and I can think of a whole bunch of ways that an extended stay can make the ice a lot thinner than usual.

Hayden's sure to get over his hero worship of Brad when he's got more than a week to work on it. And the evil twin will force the good Hayden to wear the evil-twin mask for the whole time. I'm not sure how Brad will react.

It's weird—and I have to tell you that I'm getting good and tired of all the epiphanies; you'd think they could spread themselves out at least a little—but Hayden was a perfect child the whole five years the three of us lived together.

But, then again, Hayden has basically been a perfect child for ten and a half of his eleven years. It's only in the last few months that he's exhibited any signs of being a *real* boy. So maybe that epiphany isn't one at all.

Phew. Two epiphanies are enough. In fact, I'd be perfectly happy to go through the rest of my life without having another. They're too stressful and involve way too much possible change.

Back to the potential problems posed by Brad's lengthy visit.

Hayden's bad attitude and Brad's unknowable response top the list, followed very closely by Brad's reaction to being asked to spy on my father.

I know exactly how he'll respond to *that* request.

He won't like it one little bit. But he'll do it once he sees how worried Mom is.

And there's something to be thankful for in the mess my summer has become. Mom will treat Brad exactly as she has since the day they first met. And he'll do the same.

The two of them might be brother and sister if there were siblings who never fought, who understood just when to talk and when to be silent, who never judged each other, who always, no matter what, thought one another perfect.

I don't have that kind of relationship with anyone and I envy Brad and Mom for it. But thinking of their closeness makes me think of T.J., and that brings me back to the possible disasters.

T.J.'s right up there on that list. She still doesn't believe me, no matter how many times I've said it, that I told Brad to go. When she speaks of him—which is rarely—she calls him the-rotten-bastard-who-deserted-you-in-your-hour-of-need.

I say, "What need?" but she doesn't answer, doesn't need to. Because, although I never admit it out loud and try pretty damn hard not to admit it to myself, either, I'm pretty sure that T.J. knows how I still feel about Brad. I'm pretty sure Mom does, as well.

But we don't have to talk about it. And I don't want to. Not now. Not ever.

Hayden? I don't think he cares. No, that's wrong. Let

me rephrase that. I don't *want* to think he cares, because if he does, well, it means that I might have made the wrong decision.

Which I already know—or at least the part of me in the rearview mirror does. Yes, I made the wrong decision when I told Brad to go without exploring any other possibilities except living my stupid Gidget life in Halfmoon Bay.

So if T.J. and Mom and Hayden know, why have I kept my feelings secret all these years?

I'm not even going to get into why I made the decision in the first place and I'm *absolutely* not going to try and fix it now.

Because how could I?

I have no idea how Brad feels about it, about me. He handles our meetings, the weeks we spend together, as if we were distant cousins, acquaintances, really, who see each other once or twice a year and never go further than that.

Oh, once in a while I catch him looking at me as if he'd like more, but the minute he catches me looking back, he turns away and starts talking to Hayden. Or Mom. Or Dad. Or whomever happens to be standing in the room with us at the time. And if there's no one, he makes an excuse and leaves.

So maybe he still wants me, but does he still love me? I have no idea.

That was part of the deal we made when he left. We

didn't ever talk about it, but somehow we decided to pretend—at least I'm pretending—that we are just, have really always been, only good friends who happened to have the world's most mind-blowing sex (that's my input, not his).

And now we have a child together. Small complication, I know, but we have worked very hard at working around that.

I guess I've been trying to keep the love-of-my-life-mind-blowing-sex thing a secret from myself.

And it's just not working anymore.

A case of very bad timing.

CHAPTER 12

The Prince of Tides

While I've been thinking, Hayden has vanished up the stairs. I hear the sound of the world-building game and know that he won't hear a word I say when I phone T.J. and Mom.

I'm pretty sure I could scream, a rabid Stephen King dog could appear and start howling in the kitchen, a giant could rip the roof off the house or the sky could fall and Hayden wouldn't hear it.

His powers of concentration rival Brad's. And I definitely don't want to follow that thought too far.

But I'm not ready to make the phone calls. Dealing with Hayden was one thing, and I already screwed that up. Dealing with my mother and especially T.J. is another. So if I can't make the phone calls, it means I either clean the oven—and it's tempting—or I go out to the studio for another shot at the damn cat plates.

I choose, only because there is no oven cleaner in the jumble of cleaning products under the sink, the studio.

Before the summer hit the Sunshine Coast—and hit is what it does, bringing with it a tsunami of tourists—I spent every minute here.

Before I knew about the drive-in closing, before I had my epiphanies, before Hayden's evil twin showed up, I worked. And I enjoyed every minute of it.

I have always loved the process, from conception to design to the clay between my fingers to the painting and glazing and firing. I have loved it all and considered myself a lucky woman to make a living doing work I loved.

"Summer's coming," I told myself. "Time to get ahead." And I did.

I made huge quantities of every kind of piece so that when some store reordered, I could just pick it up off the shelf and send it out. I made, for the very first time, enough pieces for all the summer craft fairs ahead of time.

I wanted, I thought while I was working those long and hot and tiring days, to spend my summer with Hayden rather than in the studio twelve hours at a time. And I was glad I'd done it when I got the order for the damn cat plates.

"Lucky," I said.

"Lucky and well-organized," T.J. said when I told her about it. "Though I was the one who suggested it, so you can't take all the credit."

"Yeah, yeah," I said back in May. Now it's well into July

and I know she's right. If I hadn't done all that work, my business would be spiraling into the toilet.

I got ahead and then…

The evil twin showed up. And the owners of the drive-in announced it was closing. And T.J.'s father was getting evicted, and my father was losing his mind.

And then I started having epiphanies.

And besides all that, the damn cat plates are blocking my creativity. I've never made more than two or three of anything, not ever.

You accepted the money, a voice says in my head.

It isn't really a voice, of course, although it's easier, mostly, for me to pretend it's someone else, some unknown being.

It's the woman in the rearview mirror, the half of me that won't allow ignoring of epiphanies or responsibilities or unwanted truths.

I did accept the money.

So you're going to have to make the plates.

I know.

And soon.

I shrug my shoulders. I hate this, I really do. The studio has been my refuge ever since Dad helped me build it. I come here when I'm sad, tired, unhappy—or happy. And it doesn't matter how I feel when I walk in the door; once I'm in, I create something.

And now I can't.

And pretty soon I won't have the drive-in, either.

I sit down with a thump and I start spinning. The office chair—a hideously mottled dirt-brown I inherited from T.J. that now has paint and clay and other anonymous flecks embedded in it—is a great spinner. It's lost all of its stopping power, so when I set it turning it pretty much keeps on going. All it needs is the occasional light nudge from a foot.

Dizzy, I keep spinning. I want to spin away all the worries, the epiphanies, the damn cat plates and the drive-in, spinning away the way wet clothes in a dryer spin away the moisture.

I spin until I feel sick, just on the verge of vomiting. And when I stop, the studio continues to whirl around me. I clap my hands over my mouth and close my eyes. I quickly snap them open again.

Throwing up is probably the worst feeling in the whole world. I'll do almost anything to avoid it, including once, when I had a bad bout of the flu, lying in a dark room without moving a single muscle for forty-two hours.

Mom thought it extreme.

"You'd get better sooner if you'd just throw up," she'd said. And she was probably right. But I didn't change my mind. Not even eighteen hours of labor was as bad as those two days.

I sit on the chair and I wait for the world to stop spinning. Sometimes when I do this I get ideas—for a new series of plates or bowls, for a new marketing scheme, for a birthday or Christmas present for my father, who is impossible to buy for.

Which is weird, really, because he loves every single thing I've ever given him. He still has the ashtray I made for him in fourth grade even though he's never smoked.

Procrastinate much?

The voice speaks over the receding nausea.

If you're not going to work on the plates, go make your phone calls.

The voice is right. I head back to the kitchen and start with Mom because she's sure to be easier.

"Mom? Where's Dad?"

"It's Monday, dear. Where else would he be?"

"Cribbage at the club?"

At least that hasn't changed. Missing the drive-in on a Saturday night was bad enough. Dad skipping cribbage would mean the world as I know it had ended.

"I've got good news."

I learned my lesson with Hayden. No more of this "I need to talk to you" or "It's about Brad" business.

"Brad'll be here in a couple of weeks."

My mother's sharp inhalation is a sure sign of her pleasure, as is her silence. Like me, she tends to talk over bad spots, but she goes silent with joy.

"He's going to stay all summer. With Hayden and me."

Mom sighs and says, "I'm glad." She pauses. "And it'll be good for Hayden."

With those words I realize that Hayden hasn't been his old self with his grandparents, either. I've spent the last few weeks holding that thought as something positive—thank goodness, I'd think, Hayden is having a good time at their house. But now I see that Mom, at least, has made the acquaintance of the evil twin.

"He's going through the terrible twos." My response is weak, I know, but it's all I have to offer.

"I know," Mom says, her voice as gentle as it is familiar. "He's just a little late. No surprise, really. He's been early with everything else."

"I think having Brad around for longer than a week will be good for him."

"For you, too."

"Maybe," I say, trying to ignore the wellspring of feelings that overwhelm my common sense each time I think of Brad in this house for weeks at a time.

"He'll take Hayden out so you can work." On the word *work* her voice wobbles a little.

I often forget how perceptive my mother is. I think it's because of the endless retelling of my conception story. She doesn't know—or she doesn't care, and I'm not sure which would be worse—that hearing about my father's sex life drives me crazy.

But in most other things she catches on faster than fast.

"It's okay, Mom. Once Brad gets here I'll have more time. The summers are always tough with Hayden home. And then there's all the craft fairs. And the heat."

Heat is a real problem for potters. It's hot enough in my studio the rest of the year—the kiln adds ten or twenty degrees to whatever the outside temperature might be—so in the summer, like a restaurant kitchen, it's often unbearable.

"Of course the summers are tough," Mom agrees.

"Gotta run. I need to phone T.J. and tell her before she hears it from someone else."

This is always a possibility on the Sunshine Coast. Even though I've only told Hayden and Mom, there's something in the air here that seems to pick up sound waves.

"How about I come over and stay with Hayden? You girls go out to lunch."

I can't think of any reason to say no to her except for the guilt I feel about the damn cat plates and I don't seem to be able to work on them, anyway.

T.J.'s up for lunch, so I tell her I'll meet her on the dock by the Sand Dollar Motel.

"And take off those stupid black panty hose before you get there. It's too hot. I'll bring you a pair of shorts and a T-shirt. You can change when you get there."

She snorts a reluctant acquiescence and says, "One o'clock okay?"

I agree and wander over to the Way-Inn to pick up food for the picnic. There's food in my kitchen, but I need to talk to the gossip queens about money for T.J., which I've forgotten about until now thanks to all the epiphanies and Brad and Hayden and my father losing his mind.

The Way-Inn is packed when I arrive, but it's mostly tourists—I know because I only recognize half a dozen people. In the winter, I recognize everyone, at least to say hello to.

"Tuna salad," I say to Rose, then add, "for T.J." so Sam'll add two extra dollops of mayonnaise and skip the green onions. "Four Diet Pepsis and an egg salad for me. Two orders of fries."

"I know—" Rose smiles "—extra salt and vinegar. I've been selling you two fries for twenty years and I swear you've downed an ocean of vinegar since then."

She peers at me over the top of her glasses. "Doesn't seem to have pickled you at all." She touches my cheek, and even though she must be almost the same age as me, she feels infinitely more wise, more settled, more of everything. "Still as soft as ever," she says, then nods at the booth in the back.

"Mercedes and Doris are back there already, and I'll be over in a minute." She looks at me more carefully this time. "I'll tell Sam to have the food ready in fifteen minutes."

I nod and don't even think to question her knowledge. The gossip queens very seldom ask questions. They're like what I imagine psychiatrists to be—at least the ones I've seen in the movies, but without the short skirts and long red fingernails—they wait for you to both ask and answer the questions.

"Hey, Doris. Mercedes." I'm being as nonchalant as I can be as I slide into the booth opposite to the two senior queens. I wait while Rose sets a sweating glass of soda in front of me and slides in on my side of the booth, effectively cutting off my escape.

I want to talk to them about T.J., but I know that in coming here I'm taking a big risk. The gossip queens have their own agenda and they may start asking questions I don't want to answer.

"How are the damn cat plates going?" Mercedes grins and I know she's asked the question just to shake me up. I forget to wonder how she knows what I call them.

"Not well," I say because there's no point in lying to the gossip queens. If I do, someone is sure to mention that my kiln hasn't been fired up for weeks or that they've seen me lolling about in the backyard most days.

I steel myself for interrogation gossip-queen style, but it doesn't happen.

"How's the baby?" Rose asks Doris.

"She is fine, walking like you would not believe. I can no longer keep up with her, so it is a good thing that Tonika is better."

Rose and Mercedes both smile at that—they had spent a great deal of time last year looking after Emily and Tonika—and then continue on with their conversation, talking about their families and friends and the summer in general. They include me in the conversation with glances and grins, but I'm not required to speak. Not until Doris—today's ringleader—swivels her dark eyes toward me.

"We have not seen you here before this," she says, her voice with the faint Japanese accent soft in tone but decidedly strong while waiting for my response.

"Except for the day she came in with T.J.," Rose reminds her.

"Yes," Doris replies, "but she sat away." Her arms encompass the rest of the Way-Inn as if it really didn't count, not compared to *this* booth.

"I think, though," Mercedes says, taking up the torch, "that what she has to say isn't about the damn cat plates or that cute boy of hers. It's not even about Bill and the Internet or how she's going to cope with her sexy ex-husband for a whole summer."

Damn my mother. She was probably on the phone to Doris the minute I hung up. Small-town gossip beats satellite information any day. I think the government should hire these women to supplement their spy service.

"It's about T.J., right?" Rose asks, delighted at being the first to say it.

The gossip queens are a lot of things. One of the main things is competitive.

I agree. "It's about T.J. She's going to need some money to buy that apartment for her dad. And I know every penny she has is tied up in the new agency and that piece of property she's bought to develop."

"You do not want her to lose it," Doris says, certainty in every word.

"No, and I have extra money." I glance at Mercedes. "Because of the damn cat plates."

"She won't want you to give it to her, but—"

"You can invest in the property," Mercedes interrupts. "T.J. makes money with everything she touches."

"You can be her partner."

The three women exchange glances I can't decipher, until I remember Mom telling me that Rose and Doris lent money to Mercedes so she could buy the Sand Dollar.

"How do I do that?"

"Just tell her the truth." Rose picks up her apron and scoots out of the booth to go back to work, her contribution complete.

"Not all of the truth," Mercedes adds. "Just that you've got this extra money and you want to invest it."

Doris ends the consult abruptly. "We have another problem to deal with now. Go have lunch with T.J."

CHAPTER 13

Wall Street

T.J. and I meet on the dock at the Sand Dollar ten minutes later. I'm carrying bags of food and soda, a blanket from the car, clothes for T.J. to change into. She's carrying nothing, but she has taken off her panty hose, though she's still wearing her heels, a short black skirt and a peacock-blue silk blouse.

I thrust the clothes into her arms and hold up the blanket. We've perfected this technique of changing in public over the years and it only takes about sixty seconds before she steps out from behind the blanket wearing my shorts and T-shirt. They're too big—she's thin as a light pole—and too short. She's almost six inches taller than me. But she looks good in them. Relaxed.

She hands me her neatly folded skirt and blouse, steps out of her shoes and flaps the blanket twice before laying it down on the warm planks.

I add the bags of food and the sweating cans of soda and sit down beside her.

This is one of our favorite places—and Mercedes is happy for us to use it. Having us here keeps the kids away, and she doesn't have to keep an eye on us. I think she figures if we drown, it's our own fault and no responsibility of hers.

T.J. bites into her sandwich. "What's up? We never do this anymore."

"I need to talk to you."

"Aimee? Is everything okay?"

I've blown it again. Everything went so well with Mom and then the gossip queens that I thought this would be fine, as well. Except for one small problem: I'm an idiot.

"It's fine. Everything's fine." I smile and hand her a soda. "I'm just an idiot."

"True. But you still scared me."

"I'm sorry."

"Okay, but don't do it again. What do you want to talk to me about? Hayden? I know it hasn't been easy this summer."

"Not Hayden. Not Dad, either." I forget I haven't talked to her about my dad.

"What's wrong with him? I saw Bill yesterday and he looked fine."

"I promise I'll tell you all about it in a few minutes, but I need to ask you something else first." I cross my fingers behind my back and hope for the best. "You know all that money I got for the damn cat plates? I think I need to invest it."

"Good idea."

I see the possibilities and the plans for my money and my future riches swirling around in T.J.'s head, so I stop her.

"Wait. I want to invest that money in your development. I want to be part of that project."

She looks at me with such an odd expression on her face that it takes me several moments to decipher. She's stunned, that's obvious, but she's also flattered that I think she's capable of making money for me. And underneath all that, she's happy. Because she'll be able to help her dad and me at the same time.

Because I've read all this on her face, I don't wait for her to answer me, I just hand her the envelope with the check in it and ignore the tears in her eyes.

"Send me the contract. I'll take it over to the lawyer's to look at it."

"Good idea," she says again and then her eyes widen with surprise at something over my shoulder.

I hear boots on the dock. I know those footsteps and I don't even turn around.

"That's the other thing I meant to tell you," I say. "Brad will be around for the rest of the summer."

CHAPTER 14

Easy Rider

I wait for Brad to arrive at the end of the dock before I turn to him, shading my eyes but still not seeing anything more than the shadowed figure silhouetted against the sun. He's positioned himself—probably on purpose, I think—with the sun at his back, so all I see is black.

"Aimee," he says, his voice as dark and rich as his shadow. "T.J." It lightens up a little when he says her name.

"Who told you?" I ask.

"I stopped at the Way-Inn. I wanted to see you before I went to the house."

All sorts of frightening ideas race through my head, things I never thought of when he said he was coming for the summer. Has he had an accident? Is he sick? Is that why he doesn't want me to see his face?

He laughs and says, "Stop it. Everything's fine, I just didn't want to barge in when you weren't expecting me."

Brad knows me too well. So does T.J.

She stands up and brushes off her—my—shorts.

"Brad. Great to see you." And she has her voice so well under control that I'm betting Brad can't hear the unease in it. I'll have to call her later—and not too much later or she'll be hammering at my door come morning.

"Same," Brad says and steps out of the sun to give T.J. a hug, which she submits to with more grace than I would have expected.

"Call me," she says and I nod. "I'll drop off the contract on my way home."

We watch as she hurries up the dock, already shedding the relaxed T.J. and transforming in less than twenty feet to her business persona. It doesn't matter that she's wearing too-short shorts or a too-big T-shirt, she's ready to sell anything to anyone.

"She looks great," Brad says as he sprawls on the blanket beside me, plucking a soda from the bag. "She looks happy. She get rid of that miserable husband of hers? He hasn't been around for a while."

"No, but I think she is happy."

I often forget that Brad knows more of what happens on the Sunshine Coast than I tell him. I forget that Mom e-mails him two or three times a week and that she knows almost as much about what goes on around here as the gossip queens do. I forget that Hayden e-mails him every day. And Dad—now that he's figured out about the Internet—probably e-mails him, as well.

My weekly note about Hayden's well-being is probably only the tiniest part of what Brad hears about Halfmoon Bay and its inhabitants. The tiniest part of what he hears about my life and Hayden's.

Another epiphany hits me.

He's home because of Hayden and the damn cat plates. And Dad. He's home because he thinks we need him. He won't admit it, but I know it's true.

"You look good, too. A little on the frazzled side, though. What's up?"

I close my eyes and pretend that I haven't just figured out that he knows *everything* that's happening to me and Hayden and Dad and T.J. And while my eyes are closed, I try not to think about how good he looks on this dock.

He's tanned—always is—and the new lines on his face just give him character.

I look up the hill to the parking lot. "Where's the bike?"

"I sold the Indian just before I left. Travel faster without it. And I had this feeling…"

"What kind of feeling?"

He touches the back of my hand for a moment, light and sure. It's the first time he's touched me in years. We're always very careful to avoid contact, always very careful not to be in the kitchen or the hallway or any enclosed space at the same time.

It feels good. And scary.

"A feeling. Like I needed to be here."

I know Brad's feelings. He believes in instinct, in doing what feels right. He believes, like Mom—and why have I never seen that before?—in spontaneity. And it seems to work for him.

He felt we needed to get married, to have a child, to travel the world. I went along.

I went along as long as his feelings coincided with mine. And then, even though they'd been right so far, I ignored them.

This is all part of my epiphany, I think. *This is all part of the change that's coming.*

"Damn," is what I say out loud.

Brad laughs, and soda spurts from his nose and all over my clean T-shirt.

"God, you're more like Hayden every day," I say while trying, unsuccessfully, to wipe the soda from my shirt and then give it up, leaving it to stick against my skin. Worse things have happened to my clothes in the studio. And with Hayden, for that matter.

"What's up, Aimee? What do I need to know before I see Hayden and your mom and dad?"

I close my eyes again and try to marshal my thoughts

into some kind of order. Obviously I keep them closed too long, because Brad interrupts the marshaling.

"Come on, we'll go for a drive."

All of our important conversations have taken place in a car—sometimes moving, sometimes not. Brad knows I find it easier to talk sitting side by side, looking out through a windshield.

"It's all those years at the drive-in," he says, managing to keep any hint of the many things that happened to us, between us, at that drive-in from his voice. "It's the place you feel safest."

I consider that for a moment.

"I guess it is," I say, reluctant to admit it but forced to by its obvious truth. I *do* feel safe at the drive-in and, by extension, in a car. Safe enough, at least, to have the awkward conversation I need to have with Brad.

Not awkward because of Hayden—that's just kid stuff. And I mean that literally. Even if Brad hadn't arrived for the summer, Hayden would grow out of the terrible twos, hopefully without growing right into some teenage equivalent weirdness.

Awkward because of Dad. I need help to figure out what he's doing. I can't solve it unless I know what *it* is and, even so, I'm scared to death that once I figure out what it is, I'll also figure out that I can't fix it.

Brad is a straight shooter—one of the reasons everyone

calls him to evaluate and fix that bike they found in some lost motorcycle graveyard, the bike they know is The One, the one they've dreamed of since they were kids. That's the reason talking to him about Dad, asking him to spy, won't be easy.

I decide not to deal with that problem now. Maybe Brad, once he spends some time with Mom and Dad, will see that something's wrong without my saying anything. And maybe, just maybe, he'll come up with a way to solve it that I haven't thought of.

"You didn't rent *this?*" I ask, coming up to a candy-apple-red 1967 Mustang convertible. It's exquisite and I crave it. I've never had a car I loved, but this could be it.

"Nope. I bought it. A summer on the Sunshine Coast without a convertible?"

Brad knows that I don't want Hayden on a motorcycle, not yet. The boy is already dreaming about them, his room filled with magazines and posters of bikes. But I don't want him—not even with Brad, the safest of drivers—on a bike yet. Nice of Brad not bringing the bike. Smart, too. Now he and I won't spend all summer fighting with Hayden about riding on the back.

Brad looks down at his long legs with a wry grin. "And those tiny new sports cars definitely don't fit."

I grin back and hop in. I don't worry at all that Brad's overspent or spent foolishly. Brad's like T.J. He understands money and investments as naturally as he breathes and fixes bikes. It won't matter what college or university Hayden chooses—Harvard, MIT, the Sorbonne—Brad's already put away enough money for any of them.

The husky roar of the engine, the wind in my hair, the low sound of Yo-Yo Ma coming from the speakers relax me to the point I'm ready to talk.

About Hayden at least.

Brad listens, smiles as I describe the chore it is to decipher our son's sullen face, nods when I reassure myself that it'll be over soon and wisely offers no slurs or suggestions about my parenting. Not that I thought he would.

He's never done that, never once said that I made a wrong decision, or that he thinks I should deal with Hayden differently, or that he knows better.

Remember? *Perfect* ex-husband.

Next I'm willing to talk about the damn cat plates or nothing.

Here Brad does offer some advice.

"I'll take Hayden off your hands. It may be all you need is a break." He stops there and I nod. But yes isn't the right answer.

"That won't help," I say. "Mom and Dad have had him for days and days and I still can't get to it. I'm blocked."

I can't believe I say that out loud, that I've admitted it

to anyone. But Brad—maybe because of his empathy—always pushes me further than I'm willing to go. He doesn't do anything overt except try to help me, and then I tell him everything.

Time to shut up, I say to myself. *Time to stop talking.*

So I start to chatter, which is what I always do when I don't want to talk.

I chatter about what's going on in Halfmoon Bay, who is getting married, who is moving, the new people, the old people, the new restaurants and the new school.

And that leads me, without planning, right into the Halfmoon Drive-In.

"I know you'll think this is stupid. Even I think it's stupid. More than stupid, really."

He raises his eyebrows and waits.

"It's closing."

I blink back the tears. I should be used to the idea by now. I just don't know what I'm going to do once it's gone. I can't imagine my life without the drive-in.

I try to explain this to Brad.

"Think about something you've done every single week of your life."

"Shaving? Brushing my teeth? Having a shower? Although, come to think of it, there have been a few weeks…" He smiles at me.

"Please. You know what I mean."

"Riding a bike somewhere? There isn't anything. There's nothing I've done every single week of my life. Every week is different."

"There has to be something."

"You mean besides those unavoidable bodily functions? Eating, breathing, sleeping, taking a—"

I interrupt him. Brad has spent too much time with Hayden, whose favorite jokes are always about farting or some other form of potty humor.

"No. Not those things. I don't know…Sunday dinner with your grandparents."

"They all died before I was born."

"Watching *Hockey Night in Canada* with your dad."

"My father drank on Saturday nights. And most others, as well."

"Oh."

Yet another thing I don't know about Brad Mackey.

"How about when you went to high school? The soda shop or track and field or…"

"Nope."

Brad pulls the car into the beach parking lot and switches it off.

"Aimee, I've never had the kind of life you have except when I lived with you. I swear I don't remember any two days that were the same, let alone over a long period of time. I just didn't—don't—do that."

Right. I remember. Brad's enamored with change. And I'm stuck in my little Gidget world.

"Damn," I say again. "You can't understand this."

"Try me."

I start again.

"You know that Yeats poem? *The Second Coming?* Where he writes 'Things fall apart; the centre cannot hold'? That's how I feel—as if I'm spinning out of control because I've lost the center."

Brad looks at me, his eyes bright with concern.

"It's as if everything I am, everything I've ever been, is vanishing with the Halfmoon."

I turn away to look at the water.

"And then," I say, "there are the damn cat plates."

CHAPTER 15

Hello, Dolly

I'm very good at changing the subject, and Brad is very good at realizing just when I've had too much.

He goes along with talking about pottery. For a guy whose life is about mechanics, tools and bikes, he's got a great eye for art. He often sends me digital photos of something he likes particularly or something he thinks will interest me.

So we sit looking out at the water—*not* at each other—and talk about pottery until Brad stops me right in the middle of a discourse about Japanese raku-yaki.

"Where's Hayden?"

"He's at home, I think. Mom's with him wherever he is."

"He knows I'm coming?"

"Hmm, though I told him you'd be a couple of weeks."

"Good, it'll be a surprise then. Come on, let's get going," he says and turns on the car.

"Okay." Because what else am I going to say? He wants to see Hayden and Hayden wants to see him.

Me? I just want to get through the summer and I want to get started on the damn cat plates. But having Brad in my house doesn't seem as though it's going to make it any easier—now I have one more thing to worry about.

Maybe I should send back the deposit? But I can't—I've given it to T.J. Maybe I should… Maybe I should just lock myself in the studio for a couple of days.

I'll fire up the kiln, I'll blow up the photos of the earlier cat plates and put them on the wall and I'll sit right in the middle of the floor and meditate on the damn things until I can see another plate. And then I'll make it.

How hard can it be?

No harder than driving up to my house beside Brad and realizing that I've forgotten my car at the Sand Dollar. Totally forgotten it. Brad Mackey could make me forget my head if it wasn't attached, I swear it.

"Brad? I have to go back down to the Sand Dollar and pick up my car."

He looks at me, then turns his head to check the driveway and the curb. There is no other car on the block except his brilliantly red Mustang—everyone must be at work or their cars must be in their garages.

"He's not here," I find myself saying. "Mom's car isn't here." As if I know what he's thinking. And I do.

He won't drive me back to the Sand Dollar if it means it'll be even a few more minutes before he sees Hayden.

But if Mom's not here, then Hayden isn't, either. And we have no idea where they might be.

They could be anywhere.

At the Way-Inn, although Brad was there and they weren't.

At the beach—any one of the dozens of beachy places within a few miles.

At the park.

At the provincial park, hiking up to the waterfall.

At the dahlia nursery, buying more dahlias for Mom's garden.

At the movies.

Dad might be with them, might not. He might know where they are, might not.

I can see all of this going through Brad's mind before he pulls into the driveway to turn around and head back down to the Sand Dollar so I can get my car.

I'll give him Mom's cell phone number when we get there because, no matter where she is, she always answers her cell phone. I've given up calling on the house phone. Dad won't answer it, and Mom's completely converted to cellular technology—that way, she won't miss a thing.

Mom's social life is extremely complicated. She plays bridge, she's a member of the lawn-bowling league, she's on the library board and she's this year's chair of the Shelter Ball.

And that's just the start of it. I can't keep up with it and

I don't know how she can, especially since she's espoused spontaneity in her life. But she never misses a meeting or a game, never keeps anyone waiting and seems able to convert from her relaxed home self to her this-is-the-general-speaking self without any trouble.

My mother could be one of the interfering mamas in a Jane Austen novel. She could be one of the gossip queens. Or a matchmaker. Or a social organizer par excellence. She could even be a psychic. She could plan parties for the queen or the president.

She could—and does—do anything. And does it well.

I wish I could do the same, but right now all my selves seem to be confused and not capable of much of anything.

The drive back down the peninsula to the Sand Dollar seems much longer than the drive up to Halfmoon Bay, maybe because we're not talking. I'm not talking because I don't want to get into any of the things I'm avoiding; Brad's not talking because he had his heart set on seeing Hayden and he can't.

"Brad?" I can't stand to see him like this. One of the things that attracted me to him in the first place was the energy he always projected whether he was happy or sad or angry or just tired.

Brad's energy poured off him, surrounding me and everyone around him with a pool of zeal that no one could resist. But now that part of him has vanished.

"I'm going to call Mom on her cell phone, okay? She and Hayden could be anywhere, but wherever they are, you can be there in half an hour."

He smiles for the first time since we left the house and I can't help myself. I smile back and then touch his thigh.

Stupid. Stupid. Stupid.

I pull my hand back and hold it, tingling, in my lap. What was I thinking?

I was thinking that seeing Brad look so dejected was a shock, so far from his usual expression that I wanted to make him feel better. Duh.

Maybe make him feel better and make me feel—what? As if I'm not some weak, helpless female who goes running to her *ex*-husband for help when life isn't going so well?

I shake that thought from my head and occupy myself with dialing Mom's cell phone.

"Hey, darling, how are you?"

I swear that Mom replaces her cell phone every six months. She's so up on the technology that I can't even imagine what this phone has—except that I know it has call display, a camera, games and video streaming. And I know this because I hear Hayden in the background.

"You can't answer the phone when I'm playing," he says.

Mom doesn't bother to put her hand over the mouthpiece when she answers, "Can so. It's *my* phone."

"But you let me play with it."

"Aimee? Can I call you right back? I have to arm wrestle with Hayden for the phone."

I laugh and hang up.

"It sounds like they're having fun," Brad says. "He doesn't sound sullen at all."

"I know." And I don't even need to look in the rearview mirror to feel the huge grin that's lighting up my face. "It's great. I only told him this morning that you were coming."

And he sounds like his old self—at least with his grandmother. That may not be true with me, but still it does my heart good to hear him sound so normal.

We sit in the car, the sun warm on our bodies, the water shot through with diamonds, and wait for Mom to phone back. I don't feel great—haven't really for the whole summer—but I feel ever so slightly better.

I feel as if I might be able to start the damn cat plates and as if Brad's visit might be exactly what Hayden needs. I try not to be too optimistic, because I won't know about either thing—not until tomorrow when I have a chance to get into the studio and see what happens.

But for the first time in a long time, I can sense the clay in my hands. And now that I can, I realize how much I've missed that sensation.

For all of my grown-up life, I've spent part of every day with my hands in damp clay, molding life from it. It has been the core of my being.

That and the drive-in.

Losing both of them at the same time has been too much for me. I've prided myself on my ability to cope with loss, but now that I think about it, maybe that's because I've never had much loss to cope with.

I never knew my grandparents—all of them died before I was old enough to remember them. My parents, both only children, had no cousins or aunts or uncles for me to miss.

Dad's allergic to dogs and cats, so I never had a pet to mourn over except goldfish and I'm not sure they really count.

Brad. That was a real loss. But it was my choice, my decision—my fault, if you will, and somehow that makes it easier to deal with.

The clay and the drive-in. No wonder I'm having a rough summer.

CHAPTER 16

The Cat in the Hat

But now I've started thinking about it, feeling it, actually feeling it in my hands, I have a craving. And it's been so long since I've had that craving that I have to go. Right now.

I can't hang around here with Brad, waiting for my mother to phone and tell us where she and Hayden are hanging out.

I hand Brad the phone.

"I've gotta go. Right now."

He looks at me as if I'm crazy, and I can't deny that maybe I am. Although frantic may be closer to the truth. Frantic to get into the studio and prove to myself that I haven't lost my abilities completely.

Frantic to get started on the damn cat plates. Because if I get started right this minute, I'm still going to be working twelve-hour days every day for the next month to get all three hundred and seventy-two done in time to be shipped for the wedding.

"Mom's going to phone. Just ask her where they are. You guys do whatever you want. I'm going to be in the studio."

There is an implicit *And don't bug me* in that statement that I hope Brad catches. If I can work, I don't want to be interrupted.

I wave as I race down the parking lot to my car. It seems to take forever to get home to the studio and fire up the kiln. But finally I'm sitting at the wheel, wet clay sliding in and out of my fingers.

But nothing's happening.

I thought I'd start off with a cup, a vase, a small bowl.

The wheel spins and the clay slides and nothing happens.

The frantic sense of possibility I felt is gone.

I can't shape even a cup.

And I've been crafting cups since I was a child. I sit back on the stool and try not to cry, try not to panic.

I remember making that ashtray for Dad. I was eleven and it was the first time I felt clay in my hands. I wanted to stay in that art class forever, feeling the soft mud of the clay turn from slush to substance.

The physical result was clumsy, but the emotional result was permanent. From that day I've thought of myself as a potter, a shaper of clay, an artisan.

And now? Now I have nothing, no feeling in my hands, no connection to the mud.

What in the hell am I going to do?

I do what I've always done when I'm unhappy, frightened or just pissed off—and today all three of those emotions are roiling around in my stomach.

I call T.J.

I get her voice mail on all four lines—business phone, private business phone, cell phone and home. I leave the same message everywhere—*T.J., call me*. Her being unreachable is so unusual it's frightening.

I can't think of another time when this has happened. And it makes me feel edgy to add to the unhappiness, fear and anger I'm already experiencing.

I power down the kiln. My concern over T.J. is pushing aside my panic over the damn cat plates, and I'm not at all sure whether that's good or bad.

But I go with it because I'm not accomplishing anything here. I'll go look for T.J. At least I'll be doing something and I won't be thinking about the damn cat plates.

Brad, Hayden and Mom haven't shown up by the time I'm ready to go, so I leave a note on the fridge—hoping that one of them will think to look there for it—because they can't phone me once I leave the house. Brad has my cell phone.

I start at the nursing home. T.J.'s dad is sitting in his usual chair, his hair brushed and his clothes tidy and clean. The attendant hasn't seen T.J. since the morning and I'm not surprised—T.J. generally only gets here once a day.

I don't really care what she did this morning. I check my watch. She left the dock almost six hours ago and no one at her office—that's the next place I check—has seen her since then.

I drive by her house. No cars, no signs of life, but I still hammer on the door, peer in through the windows, go around the back. And then I use the key on my ring to open the side door.

A cup, bowl and spoon are piled neatly in the sink and the table is spotless. I can tell she hasn't been back since the morning because the first thing T.J. does when she walks in the house after work is to put those dishes in the dishwasher—it's as inevitable as the coming of Labor Day.

Where else?

All kinds of scenarios rush through my head. I think about hospitals, kidnappers, serial killers.

Damn. I watch way too much TV. And it's way too violent.

I drive the Sunshine Coast Highway down from Halfmoon Bay toward Sechelt, heading, though I don't want to admit it, toward the hospital.

The lightly traveled highway doesn't soothe me as it usually does. The trees and glimpses of the ocean don't make me smile. Even the summer fields of red and yellow and blue flowers don't do a thing for me.

Where in the hell is she?

T.J. could have gone down to the city to deposit my check or to see her daughters. She could have gone up to Powell River to see her louse of a husband.

She has to have turned off her cell phone—that's the only way she wouldn't answer it. Because, like my mother, T.J. is wedded to her cell phone in a way her louse of a husband wouldn't understand.

And why would she turn it off?

She's somewhere she doesn't want to be interrupted. Suddenly curiosity has overpowered my worry.

Maybe the louse is toast. And maybe, just maybe, T.J. has a man. Wow. It makes perfect sense now that I've figured it out.

The louse hasn't been around for months, not really. And T.J.'s been happier than I've seen her in years.

And I *am* an idiot. Because I didn't see it, didn't notice the louse's absence, didn't notice that she was smiling more, not talking about him, that there were often hours when I couldn't find her.

I pull off at Redrooffs and hurry over to the pay phone. I leave a message on her cell phone.

"I'm over the panic. Call me when you get a chance. I'll be home tonight. Brad has my cell phone. Love ya."

I leave it at that.

The trip back up to Halfmoon Bay is the polar opposite of the trip down. I slow to contemplate the cows, horses and llamas. I stop and pick armfuls of the wildflowers growing next to the highway.

Fragrance and color fill the car, and I smile as I pull up in front of the house. Mom's car is here. The Mustang is here. And it looks as if Dad's walked over, because I see the smoke from the backyard grill. He's the only one who uses it.

T.J.'s car is pulled up to the curb and so is Rowena Dale's. Mom at her most organized.

I grab the flowers and walk through the gate into the yard.

CHAPTER 17

The Man in the Iron Mask

The party's started without me. Brad and Hayden are playing badminton—and Hayden's laughing. Mom and T.J. and Rowena are sitting on the patio, lime margaritas (my mother's favorite) in hand. And Dad is cleaning the barbecue tools.

Hayden's boom box is on the table, but his CDs aren't in it, thank God. Mom has made the selection—her summer classics CD. I know every song, from the Beach Boys and Otis Redding to the theme from *The Summer of '42.*

I smile hello and take my flowers into the kitchen. Wildflowers don't last long without water.

"Where have you been this afternoon?" I ask when I hear T.J.'s spiked heels on the tile. I don't give her time to answer. "I can't believe I haven't figured it out before now."

When I turn around, the smile on T.J.'s face almost makes me cry.

"Why didn't you tell me?"

"I didn't want to jinx it."

Okay, so I think I've figured out what's going on with her and so I must know what she's talking about, but I'm not sure enough about it to let it go without comment. "Are we talking about what I think we're talking about?"

"Let's leave it, okay?" T.J. looks around at the others and shrugs her shoulders. "Some other time."

I nod and realize that I still don't know who he is and, what's worse, I don't even have a guess. And it might not even be a man. It might be some new deal, a new agent she's scooped from another agency, one of her kids might have won an award, it could be anything.

It doesn't have to be a man.

Mom wanders back in with the empty margarita glasses, and the rest of my discussion with T.J. is postponed, partly because of Mom but mostly because we can't talk over the noise of the blender.

"Come on outside, you two. You can talk about your secrets some other time. In private." Mom crooks her fingers and we obey.

I feel thirteen again and I can see that T.J. feels the same. We grin at each other and then at Mom, and T.J. mouths, *Later*. We follow Mom out to the yard, me carrying the flowers and T.J. two margarita glasses.

For a few perfect hours I begin to believe that things

are turning themselves around. Oh, I still can't get to the damn cat plates and the drive-in is still closing, but Hayden is laughing, Dad is right here instead of hunched over the computer in his basement and I'm doing a pretty good job of ignoring my attraction to Brad.

Everything feeling just a little too perfect? You're not kidding.

All these good feelings collapse in an instant.

And it's the fault of the evil twin. Hayden has managed to subdue him right through dinner—grilled chicken and corn on the cob. He and Brad are back playing badminton when Hayden misses an easy shot.

"Shit," he yells, flinging his racket to the ground. "You did that on purpose," he yells at Brad and then stalks away.

I look at Brad, who appears stunned. Mom and Dad, Rowena and T.J. all work hard at pretending they haven't heard a thing, though none of them are very successful. They all look shocked, but they keep on talking, though I'm pretty sure that their ears are focused around the badminton net.

Now what? Do I do something? Or do I leave it to Brad? Will he know what to do?

Why should he? I don't. Hayden has stepped beyond the boundary of sullenness and into complete and utter rudeness, and I'm as stunned as everyone else.

KATE AUSTIN   129

Brad makes the decision for me. He carefully places his racket on the chair by the garage, picks up the one Hayden threw down, then the fluorescent yellow birdie. He puts them on the chair with his own.

Then he pulls out the poles for the net, unhooks and folds up the net, then carries them all into the garage. Even from the patio I hear him rattling around, putting the net and poles away. He reappears for an instant, picks up the rackets and birdie and goes back into the garage.

When he comes back out, he's empty-handed and still hasn't said a word. Neither has Hayden, who is standing in the corner of the yard far away from the patio, back to us and hands crammed hard into the pockets of his shorts.

Even from here I can see how tense his shoulders are, practically up around his ears. He isn't moving.

Poor Hayden. It must be bad enough to go through the terrible twos when you're two, but doing it at eleven? When you know what you're doing is wrong and rude and you know you're making everyone angry with you and you still can't help yourself? Poor baby.

I start up to go after him, but Brad stops me with a quiet "No. Just leave him be."

He slouches into the chair next to me and smiles around the table. "Playing badminton is thirsty work. Pass me a beer, Bill?"

Dad hands him a beer and we all start talking at once, pretending that nothing has happened.

And I'm trying hard not to apologize for my boy because he's more than old enough to know better and doesn't need me to say sorry on his behalf. Which means I'm not saying much of anything because if I open my mouth, it'll all spill out.

I'm also trying to lock myself into this chair instead of running across the grass to Hayden, where I'll either scream at him or smother him with a hug I know he'll hate.

I'm not sure that Brad has made the right choice, but it's as good as any I've made in the past weeks, so I let it go without comment and keep acting as if everything is okay while trying not to watch Hayden too obviously.

He doesn't move. His shoulders stay attached to his ears. His fists stay crammed in his pockets. He is not a happy child.

Half an hour of this and the party breaks up just as it started—without any input from me. Dad kisses the top of my head and then turns to walk across the lawn to do the same for Hayden.

Brad says, "No," again, just as softly as he did the first time. Dad turns back and heads for the car.

Mom, Rowena and T.J. follow him, as does Brad. I hear their faint goodbyes, but I can't move, not until Hayden does.

And he's still standing in the corner.

Brad drops back into the chair beside me and takes a pull of his beer. He nods toward Hayden and asks, "Does this happen often?"

I shrug. "Not this exactly, and never before in front of Mom and Dad. Not when I've been around, anyway, and not that they've told me. He's pretty moody, though, but he's been more sullen than angry so far." I shrug again. "Maybe this is a whole new phase." I try not to imagine how scary the angry phase might be.

"Ouch. It's a tough one."

"I know. But T.J. says he'll grow out of it. I've got my fingers crossed."

"It won't help to punish him?"

"Hasn't so far. He's been grounded, denied the computer and the TV, had to do extra chores. The only thing I haven't done is to put him in an iron mask and send him off to the Chateau D'If."

Brad laughs as I knew he would. Both of us loved that movie, went to the drive-in three times the week it was on. Some of those times might have been because I was staying with my parents and Brad was sleeping on the beach and it was the only way we could have a little privacy, but we did like it.

I cried every time D'Artagnan kissed the red rose and left it for his love; Brad cheered when the evil twin ended up in the mask. Both of us laughed when Porthos tried to kill himself and ended up flat on his back, still alive and kicking, the rope and a pair of boots his only clothing.

"What's on this week?"

I don't know because it doesn't matter, never has. We just see whatever's showing.

"It's the summer," I answer. "It'll either be some mediocre blockbluster or a kids' movie."

"I prefer the kids' movies myself. Is the new *Pirates of the Caribbean* considered a kids' movie?"

"I think so. Hayden wants to see it, if that counts. He's been talking about it—when he deigned to speak—all summer."

I gesture across the now-dark lawn. "Should one of us go and get him?"

Brad grimaces. "I don't think so." But he sounds uncomfortable with the decision. "What do you think?"

"I don't know. Nothing I've tried so far has worked."

Hayden still hasn't moved, the pale yellow of his T-shirt only faintly visible in the dark. I square my shoulders against the temptation to go out there and get him.

"I'm going to try the studio again. I made up your room, and there are clean towels in Hayden's bathroom." I look across the yard again. "If I were you," I say, "I'd leave him. Go watch some TV. Go to bed early. Malaysia is a long way away and on a whole different day."

Brad tilts his head to look up at me. "I am tired. I'll see you in the morning." But he doesn't get up.

I leave the two of them in the yard and I head for the studio. Maybe what I need is to work in the dark. Maybe what I need is solitude.

CHAPTER 18

The Pink Panther

The studio is as dark and as silent as I could wish—no night-lights, no hum of a computer, none of the equipment turned on so not even the faint reflection from a power button brightens the darkness.

I don't turn on a light, don't fire up the kiln or the wheel. I'm not here to work, I'm here because I can't spend another moment near my ex-husband.

The spinning chair is right where I left it this afternoon, though this time when I sit down, I don't spin. Instead I tilt it back to a dangerous degree and put my feet up on the table.

The wheels shift a bit, and I let out a tiny squeak before they stop up against a set of shelves.

I settle myself into the chair, wriggle my feet and legs until they're in exactly the most comfortable position, then I lean back and close my eyes.

I'm here by myself in the pitch-dark studio because I'm

avoiding the temptation represented by Brad, but I might as well try to get some work done while I'm at it.

Even though I didn't actually make anything this afternoon, I did get a flash of an idea while I was spinning.

Why not treat each of the damn cat plates as just that? One solitary plate? Maybe I'm blocked because I know that I have to make three hundred and seventy-two of the stupid things. Maybe all I need to do is visualize one, draw, plan and make one. Then do the next.

It'd go much faster if I could do the plates as a group, but that doesn't look as if it's going to happen. It'll take a whole lot longer—and I'm not even sure I have the time to do it this way—but I don't seem to have much choice.

I start drawing in my mind. I'm not ready to use a pencil yet.

Round plate, slight lip so that most of the plate is a single surface. A cartoon palm tree growing diagonally across two-thirds of the surface. Sun in the upper left corner, half on, half off the lip. Now for a cat. Or at least a part of a cat. A Pink Panther kind of cat—long and thin and angular. Reaching up into the palm tree.

I start humming the theme from *The Pink Panther* as I imagine that slinky cat, its long tail springing across my black plates. My cat isn't the same, but it could be the child of the Pink Panther, same elongated body, same cartoon face but a little less angular.

It's perfect.

I whip my feet off the table, propel the chair over to the wall and hit the light switch. I grab drawing paper and pencils, and quickly sketch out the plate, already seeing half a dozen variations in this one design.

I don't stop until my fingers ache, my eyes burn and I have sketched out six plates. Now all that remains to be seen is if the clay will cooperate.

If I can get the shape of the first plate right, the others will be easy. I hope. I think now that my problem wasn't the plate itself but the design. It's because I've wanted all three hundred and seventy-two of the damn things to be unique and I couldn't figure out a way to do it.

Now I think I've got it.

First thing tomorrow I'll turn on the wheel, fire up the kiln and see if I can get it right.

I spin the chair for a minute, then flip the light back off. I don't want any visitors, especially not Brad. Because if frustrated lust is what it takes to finish the damn cat plates, then frustrated lust is what it's going to have to be.

Not that I think Brad has any designs on my virtue. He hasn't made a single move on me since he left. No, it's me I'm worried about.

I always have trouble keeping my hands off him, but I've had enough willpower to manage it for a week at a time. A whole summer? That might mean—I start counting on my fingers—at least six weeks. Forty-two nights. And maybe even more than that.

The only good thing is that Brad and Hayden might go away for part of that time. And I can basically lock myself in the studio for almost all of it.

Except those Saturday nights.

Because Hayden especially will expect the three of us to go to the drive-in together. He'll expect us to borrow Dad's old station wagon with the bench seat so all three of us can sit in the front while Mom and Dad use the new truck and park next to us. He'll expect us to arrive early so we can have our regular spot and stay until the final credits have rolled right off the screen.

And that would be all well and good if it weren't for the fact that Hayden, no matter how hard he tries to avoid it, will fall asleep about halfway through the second feature.

It won't matter what the movie is. He's fallen asleep during *War of the Worlds*, *Star Wars: Attack of the Clones*, even his favorite of favorites, all three of *The Lord of the Rings*.

And that'll leave Brad and me in the smallest of dark spaces, a dark space filled with memories.

Of the first night we kissed.

Of the night he told me he thought he might be falling in love with me.

Of the night we went so far we almost went too far in public.

Of the night he asked me to marry him.

And of the night I told him he should travel without me and Hayden.

All those memories wafting through the car, choking me. All those perfect Saturday nights lingering like perfume in the summer air, trailing warmth and passion and discovery in their wake. All those memories I have trouble dealing with even when Brad's halfway around the world and I only talk to him via the computer screen.

I'm not sure I can deal with them when he's in the same car with me, our son sleeping between us, the heat and smells of the summer night blowing in through the windows.

Too many memories. Too much pain.

But, unlike Dad, I won't be able to beg off going—Hayden's too important for me to ruin his dream evening because I'm worried about my response to Brad.

I spin the chair one more time. For luck. For strength.

And then I pick up the drawings and lock the door behind me.

CHAPTER 19

Monsters, Inc.

It's too early for voices to be waking me from the kitchen. I glance at the clock. It's only nine, yet I hear two people talking from below.

One of them can't be Hayden. I've been lucky to get him out of bed by eleven all summer. Lucky that he sleeps in and grateful to be able to see him sleeping. Because when he's sleeping, the evil twin disappears—maybe taken by Sulley into the closet world.

I know I should get him up, get him out into the sunshine, force him to go to some kind of day camp or to play with his friends. But the only time he's been his old self all summer has been when he's sleeping, and I don't want to spoil that.

So I let him sleep until he finally rolls out of bed, all rumpled and cranky and sullen, and then I wait—some days, patiently, some days not—for him to go back to bed.

Okay, I know that makes me a lousy mother. I know

that I'm more than likely doing the exact wrong thing. But underneath the guilt about being a lousy mother is a deep-rooted faith in Hayden. He *is* a good boy and that good boy will—soon, please—defeat the evil twin and take Boo under his wing.

The first thing I do when I wake up is check that I didn't dream the sketches for the damn cat plates. They're real, crumpled and wrinkled from having been slept on, but they're in bed with me—*Don't go there, Aimee, just don't go there*—and they're pretty good. Even if I do say so myself.

I check the memory of the plate itself and it, too, is still there and it, too, is good.

I get out of bed in better spirits than I've been in in weeks, brush my teeth, pull my hair back into its working ponytail and stuff my body into ratty shorts and an even worse T-shirt. Even with my handsome and perfectly groomed ex-husband in the house there's no point in ruining good clothes in the studio.

I promise myself that I'll make up for it in the evenings. I'll wear long, flowing skirts—I make a mental note: *Buy some more girlie clothes*—and skimpy blouses. I'll wear my hair loose—another mental note: *Get hair styled and color the gray*. And I'll even wear perfume—*Buy perfume*.

Okay, so I've let myself go a little, but I examine myself in the full-length mirror before I go downstairs and I don't look bad. I'm tanned and healthy, and chasing after

Hayden—as well as the long hours shaping clay—means I'm in pretty good condition.

The voices are still murmuring from the kitchen, so I *know* it can't be Hayden. He doesn't talk much in the morning, certainly not enough for this lengthy a conversation, so it must be Mom. Actually, now that I think about it, I'm surprised she left so willingly last night—she loves to talk to Brad.

It's not that she wants to travel—she's quite adamant about that—it's just that she loves hearing about it and Brad is her best source. She was probably here the minute she got out of bed.

I'm right.

Mom and Brad are sitting at my kitchen table, coffee mugs in hand and Mom's favorite apple strudel ring on plates in front of them. From the look of the coffeepot and the crumbs, they've been settled in here for hours.

"Hey, you two." I grab a mug and pour myself the final cup of coffee from the pot. "What's up?"

They smile at me, twin smiles containing something more than good morning, though what it is—for some reason, I think *conspiracy*—I don't know.

"Strudel?" Mom hands me a plate and the knife. "I made it this morning. It might even still be a little warm. You didn't tell me Brad was coming yesterday or I could have brought it for dinner last night."

"I didn't know he was coming yesterday." My answer sounds a bit—okay, more than a bit—cranky, but I don't think I mean it that way and Mom pretends she didn't hear it that way.

"I didn't tell Aimee, Lily," Brad adds, "because I didn't know how long it would take me to get out of the back-country and sell the bike and I didn't want to disappoint Hayden if he was waiting for me."

She nods at Brad and ignores me. I'm used to this. My mother tells me that she and Brad have a psychic connection, as if they were siblings in a previous life.

Mom isn't interested in the psychic, the odd or the unusual in any way unless it helps her make her point—in this case, about her connection with Brad. I take her at her word. She may feel the connection, she may not, but I choose to pretend that I believe her.

Especially because she hasn't once used it to blame me for letting Brad go. She has never once accused me of being at fault, lamented that she missed her psychic sibling or complained about babysitting Hayden because I had sent his father halfway around the world.

She doesn't have to. I do it myself. All the blame she avoids, all the guilt she very carefully doesn't put upon me, I put upon myself.

Which isn't unusual.

I've been blessed with parents who believed, still do

believe, that I can do no wrong. This was good in one way: I'm an exceptionally confident adult. And bad in another: I feel all the bad things I've done and I can't get over them. If I was punished for breaking something, it'd be over. But I *still* feel as if I need to make it up to Mom for dropping her favorite bowl when I was seven.

It's one of the reasons, I'm sure, I became a potter. So I could create bowls and give new ones—beautiful one-of-a-kind bowls—to my mother. She has had my father build a big cabinet to display them. It's pretty much full.

And I feel guilty about that, too, but it doesn't stop me from making her several bowls a year.

Maybe her system works, but it forces me to carry an inordinate amount of guilt and responsibility for things that were mostly accidents. I treat Hayden differently.

If he does something wrong, he gets punished. I rely on T.J. to tell me the type and severity of the punishment each wrongdoing deserves, seeing as I don't have any personal experience.

Hidden in my locked filing cabinet in the studio—where Hayden is forbidden to be unless I'm with him—is a list of wrongful acts and suggested punishments. And even though he's eleven and I've been doing this—making the punishments fit the crimes—for a long time, I still need to refer to T.J.'s list.

That's my parents' fault. They gave me nothing to base Hayden's punishment on.

I have the list because it makes me feel better to know that I'll know what to do if something happens, though I have to admit that I've had to use only a couple of the punishments and never the most severe of them.

If T.J. had given me a punishment for sullenness, though, I'd have to admit that I'd have used it a dozen times this summer. T.J. says that some things can't be punished, they're simply part of growing up.

And that reminds me that I need to get that contract—I scrabble through the papers on the kitchen counter until I find it—over to the lawyer, signed and back to T.J., because I know she won't cash my check until it's done.

I write a short note and fax it with the contract over to the office. They'll get back to me today—the summer is always quiet for lawyers on the Sunshine Coast. I'll drive over late this afternoon, sign it and drop it off with T.J.

I pick at the apple strudel on my plate, not even trying to follow the conversation at the table. From what little I grasp, Mom and Brad are planning an afternoon—since they're taking Hayden it has to be after lunch—at the beach.

"I'm spending the day in the studio," I say, butting in without concern. "Then I have to go to the lawyer and to see T.J."

Mom and Brad both nod. Brad is the one who speaks.

"No problem. If you two want to join us for dinner…"

"Nope. I need to talk to T.J. I'll see you guys later."

Much later. The less time I spend with Brad Mackey, the better. Even my mother's presence isn't dampening the urges I'm feeling. And if her presence can't do it, nothing can.

I sense the studio and the clay waiting for me in a way I haven't for a long time, the longest dry spell I've experienced since I started making my living as a potter. And it's all the fault of those damn cat plates. Why did I make the first one in the first place?

"I'm outta here," I say and then point up the stairs. "Eleven seems to be about when he's ready to get up. I wouldn't try any earlier."

Brad's face is as expressionless as possible while Mom is wearing her whatever-you-say-dear face.

I smile at both of them. "Don't say I didn't warn you. Wake him up too early and he'll ruin your day. Guaranteed. Brad, keep my cell phone, okay? That way I can get you if I need to."

"Or I can get you," he says, and I want to read something into the tone of his voice, into the words, but I'm sure there's nothing there to read.

I mentally smack myself upside the head and warn myself yet again that Brad is no longer mine. That these stupid feelings will only serve to complicate my already overcomplicated life. That he isn't stupid and if I keep looking at him as if he's crème caramel, he's going to figure it out.

And once he figures it out, I have absolutely no idea what he'll do about it. That expressionless face he's wearing this morning? He's worn it around me for all of the past six years.

He might sit me down and have The Talk with me. You know the one. We're divorced; it's over; we need to move on; *you* need to move on.

He might continue to ignore it the way he's done since I let him go.

He might feel it necessary to move out of my house and into my parents', though I suspect that'll be at the bottom of the list. He won't want to hurt Hayden.

And he might, if I were lucky, decide to take me up on my implied offer.

CHAPTER 20

The Tango Lesson

The studio is too clean, too quiet and definitely too empty when I open the door. The only indications that I've even been here in weeks are the spinning chair sitting in the middle of the room and the slight disorder of the drawing paper.

The tidiness won't last a minute. I start messing it up immediately.

I throw the sketches down on one of the tables and pull paints and glazes from the shelves.

I add brushes and rags and buckets for mixing.

I fire up the kiln and turn the built-in air conditioner up to full blast, then add the noise and whine of the half dozen fans.

You can tell I haven't worked here in a while, because I forget to anchor the paper on the table. I quickly place broken shards of earlier mistakes onto the sketches so they won't blow away.

I turn on the power for the wheel, haul out the clay, grab a crusty apron from behind the door and put it on over my equally stained clothing.

And then I do my favorite thing—besides molding the clay itself—I head for the stereo in the corner and I begin to stack the CDs for the day. I bought a system that means I can put in a dozen CDs, more than enough to get me through the day. It's always the first thing I do. When I started out, I ruined more tapes and albums and CDs by picking them out with my clay-splattered hands. I'm more careful now.

Today the music needs to be upbeat, maybe even slightly exotic, so I start with Yo-Yo Ma's *Soul of the Tango*, then add some blues. Artie Blues Boy White and Alicia Keys. Some country—Patsy Cline and Trace Adkins—and finally, for a different spin on it all, the Blind Boys of Alabama.

Then I put it on random, turn the volume up as loud as it will go and get my hands dirty.

It works.

I hold my breath—or it seems as if I do—for the first half hour or even longer. I'm still not one hundred percent sure that I'm going to be able to do this, but after the first thirty minutes I begin to believe it might work.

The clay feels right under my palms and the plates—I try three or four variations during the morning—look good. I won't know until I've glazed and fired them, but I'm pretty confident.

Which is a whole lot better than I've been at any other time during this summer.

Lunchtime comes and goes. I pull a bottle of water from the case on the shelf under the stereo and eat two granola bars. I'm not full, not by any means, but I am capable of going on. And I want to.

I don't paint the cat design on the plates, I just glaze them with a plain pale glaze and pack them into the kiln. They're experiments and I need to know which size and shape and weight works best. If I'd known this was going to happen, I would have made an extra plate in the first place and kept it on my shelves.

But I didn't, so I'll wait and see which one works and then I'll use it for all three hundred and seventy-two of the damn things.

I don't want you to think that overnight I've become enthusiastic about this project, because I haven't. I still hate the idea of the damn cat plates, resent having to spend my summer doing basically the same thing over and over again.

The good news? They'll keep me mostly away from Brad and I won't have to watch as he charms Hayden out of the terrible twos—which will definitely piss me off even though I know it's the best possible thing for Hayden. I just wish I'd been able to do it myself.

The other good news? The only reason I'm even able

to work on the damn cat plates—at least I think it's the reason—is that I gave the money to T.J., thus accomplishing a good deed with the money for the damn things.

And that thought turns my eyes to the clock. Three-thirty. Time to get cleaned up and head over to sign the contract.

The kitchen seems sad and too quiet when I get back to the house, as if it misses the back-and-forth of Brad and Mom, maybe even Hayden's heavy footsteps and constant opening of cupboards, refrigerator and microwave oven. I turn on the radio on the counter and pick up the phone to call T.J.

"Hey, Aimee. What's up? Where's that gorgeous ex-husband of yours?"

There's more than a hint of salaciousness in T.J.'s tone, which I choose to ignore though that won't stop her.

"Working on the damn cat plates," I say.

"You're kidding."

I respond to the shock in her voice. "No, really. And they seem to be going fine."

"Good," she says, shock lessened but still there. "I'm glad. So where is he?"

"At the beach with the parents and Hayden. They invited you and me to join them for dinner, but I said no."

"Why? I could use another home-cooked meal, even one coated in sand and probably burned to a crisp."

I smile. Dad's a firm believer in well-done meat, so T.J.'s not kidding when she says burned. I shift on the stool—my shoulders and arms are aching—and continue.

"I want to talk to you."

T.J. doesn't say a word, just takes in a sharp breath.

"I want to know what's going on with you and I want to give you the signed contract."

"Okay," she says, but I'm pretty sure she's only responding to the contract part of the sentence. And then she sighs. T.J. knows when not to argue with me. "Where and when?"

"Not here. I have no idea when Hayden and Brad'll be home. And not the Way-Inn, either. It's Friday night, way too noisy."

I think about cooking and then decide against it. "How about I stop and pick up food and you stop at the liquor store and pick up tequila and margarita mix?"

The shower wakes me up from the fugue state I'm often in after a day in the studio. The drive over to T.J.'s, stereo blasting, fresh ocean air blowing through the windows, rouses me even more. By the time I get to T.J.'s, I'm feeling as good as I have for weeks.

I stick the number of my cell phone—already written on a hot-pink sticky note—by T.J.'s phone. I need to remember to call Brad if I decide to sleep here at T.J.'s, which, based on the three or four margaritas we usually have on a night like this, is more likely than not.

I mull over margaritas as I haul the bags from the restaurant into the kitchen. Margaritas are a summer treat, cold as winter and tart as a December wind. I'm pretty sure Mom got T.J. and me started drinking them, probably when she found the recipe in one of her travel magazines.

She doesn't like to travel, that's true—I don't think she's ever been farther than the mainland—but she loves to read about it, loves to watch movies and travel shows set in exotic places. And she shares all that information with us.

Unlike me, who doesn't like to travel, read about it or choose movies for the faraway settings and never turns the TV to PBS or the Outdoor Living Network for fear of finding some travel show. I like it here in Halfmoon Bay. I like knowing who's likely to pass by on the street, who's sitting at the traffic light next to me, who's in the booth beside me at the Way-Inn.

I like recognizing my neighbors and I like being one of the old-timers.

And I realize that, more and more this summer, my epiphanies or self-knowledge or just plain inconvenient random thoughts are confirming even to me, who has spent every day of my grown-up life denying it, that I, Aimee Anouk King, am Gidget and *not* film noir.

I'm not happy about it, either. It's not easy to change your self-image after thirty years, not easy to realize that the type of person you've despised—okay, that's kind of harsh, but it feels as if it's true—is exactly the type of person you are.

And once again I have absolutely no idea what, if anything, I need to do about it. But I'm in exactly the right place and with the right person. If anyone knows what I should do, it'll be T.J.

And if she doesn't know? She'll make it up.

"So why," I ask T.J. after I've gotten this far in my musings, "did I fall for Brad?"

T.J., who of course missed the lead-up to this question, looks at me as if I've lost my mind.

"Huh?" Which is a perfectly reasonable response under the circumstances.

"I'm a homebody, right? I mean, I never go anywhere, I like to know the names of everybody I see in a day. So why Brad?"

"You mean why fall in love with a guy who has spent most of his life on the road, a complete stranger? Oh, honey, you're just finally asking yourself that question?"

"Yes."

T.J.'s one of the few people I've ever talked to about my Gidget-versus-film-noir personality split. So when she says, "Film noir," to me, I understand what she's saying. I think.

But she's not finished.

"I hate to break it to you," she says, handing me a mar-garita and pushing me out onto the porch, "but I wasn't surprised about Brad, only surprised by how long it took you to do something about it."

"About what?"

Maybe T.J. started out in this conversation a little bit behind, but now she's so far past me I'm having trouble keeping up.

"You have this dichotomy going in your life. You want safe, you follow in your mother's footsteps that way, but you absorbed a whole other kind of life with those movies. So you have a craving for something else. Brad was a way to have that something else without giving up your safety."

She sips at her margarita and sighs. "It smells so good out here. I can see why you don't want to leave."

I take a deep breath along with her and hold it. There's the ocean, always and forever the ocean. And pine trees. Both scents strong and deep. Layered over them tonight are lighter, more summery smells—fresh-cut grass, barbecues and bonfires wafting up from the beach and that perfect hypnotic July aroma of roses at their peak.

"Hmm, it's lovely." But I have to get back to the point of this discussion. "Brad wasn't safe." I try to hide the whine in my voice, though I know T.J. will pick it up no matter how hard I try to disguise it.

"No, he wasn't safe, but you thought he was. He wanted to get married, settle down, raise a family. The perfect guy for you—film noir past, Gidget present."

I hate the fact that she's right, that she understands me better than I have understood my own actions.

"But…"

"And then the moment he wanted to include part of his film noir past in your present, you bolted."

Now I understand why T.J. always seems so angry at Brad. It's not really him she's unhappy with, it's me. Like Mom, she hasn't wanted to tell me, but she thinks I made the wrong decision.

I think they might both be right.

CHAPTER 21

Le Divorce

Now that T.J.'s said what she wanted to say about me and Brad, it's my turn.

"Who is he?" I go right for the jugular. T.J. didn't pull any punches, so I won't, either.

Her face reddens, I think, though I can't be sure of that with the setting sun casting shades of pink and rose-red on the yard.

"He who?" she asks, her voice as normal as if she's asking me if I want another margarita.

Which I do. I hold up my empty glass and, when she shakes her head, make my own. Very light on the tequila.

This inquisition isn't going to be anywhere near as easy as I expected it to be. I was pretty certain she'd just spill it all the minute I walked in the door, but obviously that's not going to happen. I'll just have to go at this in a different way.

"You seem so happy these days," I say, pretending to give

up on *he*, whoever *he* is. "Looks like everything's going well. The agency. The new development."

T.J.'s smile lights up the yard in a way that rivals the setting sun.

"Everything's perfect. The ads on the mainland are bringing all sorts of clients, and all those new condos are constantly turning over. I might even need to hire some more agents."

"Wow. You told me you thought it might take a year before you made any money at it."

"Six months. I've got a feeling about that, though things are sure to slow down to a near stop by October."

T.J.'s instincts about money are almost always right on, so if she says six months, it'll be six months. But that isn't enough to create the glow she's wearing.

"And the council loves the plans for the development. I should have planning board approval before September."

"Wow again. Things are really going well for you. So who is he?"

This time she harrumphs in frustration. "There is no he. I'm married, remember?" She holds up her hand with the thin gold band.

And then something extraordinary happens. The sun's lowering rays hit the band with light and then… Well, I don't believe it myself. The thin gold band snaps right in half and falls, with the faintest of tinkles, onto the porch tiles.

"T.J.?"

"What happened?"

Our trembling voices match the shiver I feel down my spine. We fall to our knees to find the pieces of T.J.'s wedding ring, but they're gone.

T.J. sits back on her heels. "It's a sign," she says, her words now strong and steady. "I'm doing the right thing."

"What right thing?" I have no idea what she's talking about.

"I kicked Chris out. That's why he's up in Powell River. I'm sick and tired of him sponging off me. And I've told the girls the same thing. I'll help them if they really need it, but I'm not sending them any more money to pay the rent because they've spent their money on trips to Hawaii or Mexico. They have good jobs. They can pay for their own vacations."

I'm stuck back on her first sentence. "You kicked the louse out?"

I've never, not even once, called T.J.'s husband *the louse* to her face, but I can't help myself. I do it again. "You kicked the louse out?"

"Almost three months ago."

"I thought he was upcoast fishing."

"I think so, but I don't really care as long as he's not here. I send him a little money every month. That's all I know. All I want to know."

"Holy cow, T.J. Why didn't you tell me this before?"

I gulp down the rest of my margarita, spasming as an immediate brain-freeze headache hits.

T.J. laughs and waits while I moan and groan and massage my temples until the intense pain goes away.

"I wasn't sure I'd be able to stick to it and I didn't want to look like a fool if I told you that he'd gone and then had to tell you he was back."

"That makes sense, I guess."

I say this, but I'm really hurt. And confused. We're best friends and she hasn't told me about her husband? Or her daughters? And it's been three months?

T.J.'s face is serene and relaxed in the golden light from the patio lanterns. I'm not sure I've ever seen her this serene—certainly not in the last few years. I tamp down my hurt.

"This is why you're so happy?"

She nods.

"No new man?"

She shakes her head.

"Time for another margarita." And I head into the kitchen to make it.

T.J. getting divorced? I can't believe it. T.J. on Brad's side and not mine? I can't believe that, either, except that it's so obviously true. And I bet my mother feels the same way—even more so because she likes Brad so much.

Talk about seeing only what you want to see. I must be the queen of avoidance.

T.J. hates Brad. She must because she's my friend. It can't possibly be that she thinks I've made a mistake.

T.J.'s got a new man. She's happy so it must be about a man. Can't be because I'm lusting after and longing for my ex-husband so I'm seeing everything in those terms.

Mom likes Brad, but she loves me more. That's why she's on my side and not his. No, that's why she doesn't take any side at all.

The blender has been diligently crushing the ice while I've been thinking and I've let it go too long. The ice is crushed right past margaritaville and into very cold and no longer slushy water. I pour it out and start again, this time concentrating on the blades as they pummel the chunks of ice.

I add the minimum amount of tequila and mix and pour the concoction into chilled and salted glasses. Margaritas aren't margaritas without salt. I don't care what anyone says about how bad it is for you.

"What are you going to do about Brad?" T.J.'s question is quiet in the stillness of the July night.

"I don't have any idea."

She giggles and looks at me, that salacious smirk on her lips again. "That's what you told me when you first met him, and remember what happened then."

"Yeah, and look what's happened since then."

I contemplate the Brad problem. There is no good solution, only survival. I just have to get through the summer.

I need to spend twelve hours a day in the studio with the damn cat plates.

I need to figure out what's wrong with my dad and I need to fix it.

Most of all, I need to figure out a way to live through the Saturday nights after the Halfmoon closes and between now and when Brad leaves.

Those Saturday nights are going to be tough, maybe impossible. They're going to test my willpower and I'm not sure it's a test I can pass.

I clench my teeth and grimace at T.J., who is contentedly sipping her margarita and watching me wrestle with my demons. She grins at me, waggles her fingers, then her toes, and grins again.

I speak the words as a prayer, a meditation, an affirmation.

"I just need to get through the summer."

CHAPTER 22

The Poseidon Adventure

Sometime later in the evening I call my cell and count myself lucky that Hayden answers rather than Brad. Given the circumstances of the last twenty-four hours, the third margarita T.J. just pressed into my hand, the emotions swirling around in wild, exotic colors in my head, it's better that I don't speak to Brad. Not now.

And maybe not for a few days. I can pretty much avoid him—hiding in the studio is a legitimate option—but it's past midnight and that means it's Saturday. Unlike my dad, I can't miss the Halfmoon.

There's Hayden—he'll know something is wrong if I don't go and he doesn't need me to be making his poor life any more miserable than it already is.

There's Brad, who isn't stupid and would guess in a moment just why it is I'm not going and who would spend the next week walking around with an insufferable smirk on his face, and I'd just keep getting more and more and more angry with him.

There's Mom and T.J., both of whom would worry big-time if I didn't go.

And finally there's my beloved Halfmoon Drive-In. I only have a few weeks left and I want to enjoy—and mourn—every one of them.

So I have to go and I have to be able to handle Brad in that enclosed space at least that one night a week.

I tape a note to T.J.'s bathroom mirror—*I'm off home. Will be in the studio all day, but I'll call you later*—because she's sure to worry when no one answers the house phone all day.

I leave the note rather than saying goodbye in person because no one except Hayden can sleep like T.J. On the weekends, if she doesn't have a meeting or an open house, she can sleep until noon, even later.

That's never worked for me. Even as a teenager I was up and out of bed early. Just call me Gidget.

I can't help it—I'm torn between laughing or sobbing hysterically as I get into my car.

I wonder why it is this happens. Why for almost all your life you go along perfectly well, knowing exactly who you are and exactly what you want. Oh, there are bumps and problems along the way—there always are—but you know you can deal with them, you know *how* to deal with them, because you know who you are and how that person deals with things.

And then one thing, one small, seemingly inconsequential thing happens and your world turns upside down in an instant.

Worse, because of that one small thing and your reluctant recognition that you're maybe not the person you always thought you were, the upside-down world stays upside down.

You feel as if you're trapped on the *Poseidon* with Shelley Winters and Ernest Borgnine and nothing makes any sense because everything is the wrong way up. You're more than confused, you're scared to death.

Because that topsy-turvyness begins to affect everything. The way you see the world, the way the world sees you. It changes your future—that's inevitable—but even more confusingly, it changes your past.

Things you were absolutely certain you'd done correctly at the time—and yes, okay, I'm talking about Brad—begin to take on quite a different appearance in light of the upside-down world you're now living in.

I'm in the car and I'm waiting for the woman in the rearview mirror to show up and start gloating. But she doesn't and now I have one small thing to be thankful for. I'm pretty sure I'd strangle her if she did show up, and then the car would crash.

I'm wearing my seat belt and I'm not traveling fast enough

for it to be serious, but if it happened, I'd have to deal with getting the car towed and repaired, getting a loaner, dealing with the insurance company. You get the picture.

No, not today. Not even this summer. I pull over to the side of the road, turn off the car, lean back in my seat and close my eyes.

"Pull yourself together," I say, knowing without seeing her that the woman in the rearview mirror is waiting for me to speak to her before she says anything.

When she does speak, I'm shocked.

Relax, is what she says. *This isn't easy, but you'll make it. I promise.*

"*What* isn't easy?" I still have my eyes closed. I know she's really only me, but she's not a me I recognize, and that makes it kind of creepy watching her—same hair, same eyes and cheekbones, same lips, but my lips aren't moving and hers are.

Changing your life, she says. *Dealing with epiphanies. But you can do it.*

"Doesn't feel like it."

I know. Maybe you should just push it to the back…

"And how in the hell am I supposed to do that? Everything and everyone is conspiring to make sure I don't have a minute to forget it."

Spend the day in the studio. And relax. You're just making it harder than it needs to be.

"Right."

Now I'm angry and I'm discovering that it's not so hard to be angry with yourself if that part of yourself is visible—even if only in a rearview mirror. Funny how we can fool ourselves, isn't it? That woman in the rearview mirror? She's not me, so it's okay to be mad at her.

I tilt the mirror up so it faces the roof of the car and drive, carefully checking both of my side mirrors. I make it home and I've almost stopped shaking by the time I get there.

Can't miss the candy-apple-red Mustang in the driveway, though the house seems quiet otherwise. It's still only seven o'clock. Even Brad won't be up this early.

The next-door neighbor's automatic sprinkler system starts up and creates rainbows of light on my driveway. I check the angle of the water. The spray reaches almost to the Mustang, but unless the wind changes—I raise my head to check the puffs of cloud floating in the blue summer sky—it won't hit the convertible.

Good. Because I'm not sure I'd have put up the top even if the sprinklers would soak the car. And I don't need any more reasons to think badly of myself.

I don't even go in the house. I'm not ready to see Brad alone, and Hayden will be in bed for hours yet. I sneak around the side, out to the bottom of the yard, and slip inside the studio without seeing anyone or anyone seeing me.

Safe.

I look down at my clothes—a brilliant orange-and-gold cotton skirt and orange silk T-shirt—and shrug. I'll put on an apron and hope for the best.

Today calls for a different kind of music. I stack up Chris Smither, Joe Cocker and Bonnie Raitt, add Dire Straits and Meat Loaf, then a smattering of Nina Simone for fun. And, as always, turn it on full blast.

The plates from yesterday are fired. No pattern yet—won't ever be on these plates: they're prototypes—but I set them down on the table and study them.

One looks and feels a bit too light, too delicate for the cartoon design, but I like it so I set it aside. I'll probably use it for something else later. Once, that is, the damn cat plates are complete.

The second is a possibility, but I think the lip isn't shallow enough. The pattern is too asymmetrical to look good on this plate. This one I put in the garbage pile. Nice try, but...

Underneath my calm, cool professionalism, I'm starting to be concerned. Only two more options and what if neither of them works? I can't start all over again. I can't.

But the third shape is perfect. I have no trouble imagining the palm tree, the cat, the sun on this plate. Suddenly I can see all the colors—black and pink, green and gold—and how they'll fill and shape the space.

The relief makes me cry. I know I was worried but not just how much until I'm no longer worried. I swipe away the tears and get started. By the time noon rolls around and my stomach growls loudly enough to get my attention, I've got twenty plates in the kiln and know I can do another twenty this afternoon.

And I've forgotten—oops—that Brad is likely to be in my kitchen.

Which, of course, is exactly where I find him.

"I was just coming to get you," he says. "Figured you'd need something to eat after that marathon."

I don't even question how he knows what time I started or how he knows that I was working rather than hiding from him.

He pulls out a stool from the island, then undoes the apron and pulls it off me. He gingerly folds it up, crackly clay side in, and takes it over to the French doors to the patio.

"I'll just leave it out here, okay?" His eyes run a quick check of my orange-and-gold clothes, but he's seen me at or after work too often to be surprised at the mess I've made of myself.

"Get changed before you go back out there." He doesn't question the fact that I will—something I've always loved about him. Bad Aimee, do not go there. Do *not*.

"And bring me those clothes. I'll see if I can save them." Another thing I've always…

A clatter of racing footsteps—Hayden in a hurry—comes down the stairs.

"What's for lunch, Dad?" His enthusiasm wanes the minute he sees me at the table.

Damn. That hurts.

I smile, though, hoping that only I'm aware of the pain underneath it, though Brad's lowering eyebrows tell me he's seen it.

I shake my head just the tiniest bit. Hayden doesn't need to see that we're conspiring. It can't help but make things worse.

"Hey," I say, pulling out the stool next to me, "how was the beach yesterday?"

"Okay," he mumbles, putting to rest any hope I might have had of sharing lunch with the old Hayden.

"Burgers are almost done," Brad comments, patting Hayden on the shoulder as he heads for the grill on the patio. He waves at the bottles and bowls on the table. "Get your buns ready."

I wait for Hayden to object. He's hated pretty much every single thing I've cooked recently, including his once-favorite burgers. He says nothing, just grabs a bun and begins loading.

Ketchup first, then mayo, mustard and relish, gobs of each of them. And if you think that's overkill, just wait. Tomatoes, fried onions and mushrooms, pickles, then a few (Hayden likes hot but not too hot) banana peppers. Cucumbers. Three strips of bacon.

He stops there. Brad will have melted the cheese on the burgers before he brings them back in.

My mouth waters as I load up my bun. Ketchup, mustard, fried onions and lots and lots of pickles. I know, I know, it's boring, but that's the way I like my burgers. Too many flavors and I can't taste any of them.

Brad and I exchange small talk about the neighbors—who's married, who's moved in or out, how many engagements Rowena's had in the past year (two, you're interested), what's up with Mom and Dad, which hits a little too close to one of the subjects I'm avoiding. Brad, astute as ever, senses the avoidance and changes the subject.

"How are the damn cat plates coming along?"

"Good," I say, my mouth full of burger. "Really good." Here's the perfect opportunity so I take it. "But I'm still going to have to put in pretty long days to finish them in time."

"But the drive-in?" The whine is only just barely audible in Hayden's voice, a good sign. Yesterday he wouldn't have bothered to try to hide it.

"We've already asked Grandpa if we can borrow the station wagon and he said yes. He's not going tonight anyway."

I ignore the pang of worry I feel at the last sentence and respond to the first.

"Drive-in is good. But that means I have to get back to

work right away." I reach out to ruffle his hair, but he jerks away—too much, too fast, I guess.

"You clean up, okay?"

Hayden looks at Brad—damn, I'm going to have to quit resenting every time that happens—and then nods. He's not happy but he'll do it.

Small improvement but better than nothing.

CHAPTER 23

Big Night

The afternoon in the studio goes well but not as well as the morning. It never does. The heat builds and I get physically tired, followed rapidly by mental exhaustion. My creativity crashes to a halt usually somewhere around three o'clock.

Based on today, I can make my deadline—just—and I might even enjoy it a little. The plates themselves are the nicest I've ever shaped, and every time I look at the designs I think of another variation.

The bride and groom and their hordes of friends and relatives are going to enjoy their gifts. And I'll bet—and I'm not sure whether to be happy or sad about this—I get at least a few orders for more plates for complete sets from some of the guests.

I'm drenched in sweat, my arms and legs are trembling, my back aches and a severe headache is hovering right behind my eyes. I've stuck this out a little too long after too many weeks away. My body has forgotten how worrying this work can be.

I can push it but not often by this much. So, instead of forcing myself to keep working, I clean up, take a quick peek out at the driveway—no Mustang—and scurry for my room.

A long, cool shower, some of my favorite body lotion—trying to convince myself that its application is another way to keep cool—a couple of Advil, then I slip into my nightshirt and into bed. An hour's rest—even if I can't sleep—will help me get through a stressful evening. And calling it *stressful* is putting it mildly.

As I drift half in, half out of sleep, I think about my father. Two Saturday nights in a row—something is up with him. And I hope it's not what I fear it is.

Dad missed the whole male midlife-crisis thing. No sports car, no change of career, no mistress or divorce. I'm not sure I even noticed the smallest of glitches in his behaviour.

But maybe he's feeling that need now. His whole life has changed in the last few years. He's retired—and though I thought he was enjoying his new and supposedly improved schedule, maybe he's not. Add that to Mom's complete lack of schedule when she followed his for so many years, and it may be he's being driven crazy.

I need to talk to Brad about more than Hayden. But as I drift off to sleep, I have only the Halfmoon in my head, no sign of either Dad or our boy. A tiny hint of Brad, but even that thought quickly disappears into the soothing pale gray of sleep.

THE SUN IS BEGINNING to pinken the sky when we finish loading the station wagon. Brad and Hayden had already picked it up, along with my mother, when I woke up out of what was more than a nap but not enough to be called a night's sleep.

I hear them downstairs banging around in the kitchen, all three of them—including Hayden—laughing, and for the second time today I find myself wiping tears from my eyes.

Of course I'm happy to hear Hayden laughing. I have to be, I'm his mother. I'm his mother and I know the minute he hears me walking down the stairs he'll stop. And I'll know for sure that the terrible twos are all about me.

And that there's nothing I can do about it.

So, as women have done in stressful situations for hundreds of years, I dress up. I put on my favorite gypsy skirt—turquoise and lime-green—and a low-necked turquoise shell. I dampen and blow-dry my hair so it fluffs out around my face into what my mother calls my Farrah Fawcett do.

I concentrate on my makeup, adding—at the last minute—lipstick and eyeliner. And then I slip on lime-green flip-flops, spritz myself with fragrance and hurry downstairs before I lose my nerve.

Brad is alone in the kitchen when I appear, and the way he looks at me is surprising although not strange, because he's looking at me the way he used to. The way he looked at me before I told him that Hayden and I wouldn't go with him, before I told him that it was okay by me if he went without us.

"You smell good," he says, leaning in just a little too close for comfort. I can feel the heat he radiates and remember—and wish I didn't—how much I enjoyed that heat.

I back off, not because it's what I want—exactly the opposite, in fact—but because it's the safe and sensible thing to do. Brad grins at me and hands me a small cooler.

"There's wine and glasses in here, so don't drop it."

He turns back to the counter and picks up another bag. "That's it. Your mom and Hayden have packed everything else."

"What about Dad?" My voice wobbles a bit and I try again, more calmly this time. "Why isn't he coming with us?"

"He said he'd seen the movie."

"That's never stopped him before." The wobble has turned itself into a squeak.

"And he had something else he wanted to do."

God, I feel as if I've turned into a fountain, because I feel the tears threatening again. I turn my face to the ceiling and try for calm. The calming doesn't work, but the tears stop prickling at my eyes.

"We need to find out what's going on with Dad," I say, hoisting the cooler to my chest and heading to the front door, my back to Brad. "Can we talk about this later?"

Implicit in this statement is that I don't want to discuss Dad in front of Mom and Hayden. Also implicit is that I need Brad's help. I know he's heard both of the implications when he speaks.

"I'll meet you on the patio after I carry Hayden up to bed."

"Unfair, Brad Mackey," I whisper so he can't hear me. "Totally unfair."

Because Saturday nights were always special for us. From the time Hayden was born we would pack him up, first in his little bed, then in a baby seat, then on the front seat with us, and go to the drive-in.

We'd watch, or not—depending mostly on Hayden's sleep and food cycle—the movies and then drive home, the baby, then the little boy, sleeping in the car with us.

From the beginning Brad was the one who put Hayden to bed, most evenings carrying the already sleeping child up the stairs and tucking him in. But Saturday nights were always special.

The day was charged with anticipation. He'd pass me in the hallway and stop, his hand touching my waist, and lean in to kiss me on that spot behind my ear that always made me shiver. I'd pat his butt in return and carry on.

In the kitchen, I'd sit down across the table from him,

toe off my shoes and wriggle my feet onto his thighs. And then, for a moment, a little higher.

This was all about anticipation, about enticement, about seduction, so we never went too far. We'd tease each other all day and then I'd go upstairs for a shower. I'd always put on something special, take care with my makeup and wear perfume.

It heightened the anticipation.

And then we'd watch the movies, Hayden between us but our hands meeting across the back of the seat, fingers caressing when passing a glass or a napkin or the tub of popcorn.

By the time the movies were over, both of us were desperate to be alone.

We'd hurry home and Brad would take Hayden up to bed. Then he'd come back down the stairs for me.

And Brad Mackey had deliberately reminded me of those nights as I'd, consciously or not, done the same by dressing up and wearing perfume—the same perfume I'd been wearing for years.

The same perfume Brad sent for my birthdays and Christmases. It didn't matter where he was, he always found it and always shipped the bottle in time to arrive at my door the day before the holiday. I haven't had to buy perfume since Brad left.

And what are the implications of that? I choose not to explore them. Not today.

As if life isn't complicated enough already. I resolve that I will not cry, that no matter what movie is showing I won't shed a tear.

In the end, my resolution is unnecessary. Because summer Saturday nights are usually kids' nights at the Halfmoon Drive-In. The double feature starts with *Ice Age: The Meltdown*, and all four of us giggle our way through the entire thing.

What's not to laugh about? A mammoth who believes she's a possum and wants to sleep hanging by her tail upside down in a tree? A cast of crazy animals and a squirrel still chasing an acorn?

Plus Brad resisted—thanks, I'm sure, to Mom's presence in the backseat—touching me in any way.

I don't even remember the second movie because I, instead of Hayden, fell sound asleep sometime during the intermission. I fell asleep despite the kids screaming in the playground, the car doors opening and shutting as people ambled off to the concession stand or the washrooms, the twenty-year-out-of-date announcements on the screen and—fifteen seconds behind—on the speakers.

I don't wake up until we drop Mom off. Drool pools on my cheek, my neck and shoulders scream in pain as I try to straighten up and my skirt is trying to strangle my legs.

Hayden, for the first time ever, is still awake when we

get home, so I don't have to shake him from sleep to get him to bed. I haven't been able to carry him up the stairs for years, though I have no doubt that Brad can.

I'm spared one more reminder of those special Saturday nights. Hayden goes up the stairs by himself and without complaint.

"Dad? Will you sleep in my bed tonight?" He holds out the sleeping bag that always goes to the drive-in with us. "I'll sleep on the floor."

Brad glances at me and I shrug. We can talk in the morning. Or anytime, really.

I'm not sure why I have such a sense of urgency about Dad. I don't think it's urgent, but I *feel* it is even though I know there's nothing I can do about it—and maybe that's why it seems so imperative.

It's yet another problem this summer that I can't solve, but somehow this one may be more manageable. I just want to fix something. The damn cat plates are going okay, but the whole ex-husband thing is getting worse, as is the drive-in thing.

I just want to solve one problem and because T.J.'s problem, even though not mine to solve, was easy, my mind, simple as it is, expects that Dad's problem—again, not mine to solve—will be fixed the minute I step in.

Stupid, right?

"Have fun, you two," I say instead of worrying any

more about Dad, "but keep it down, okay? I have to work tomorrow."

I smile at them and go up to my bedroom, thanking Hayden under my breath.

I've made it through one Saturday night, one evening of painful memories and bone-deep longing, without making a fool of myself in front of my mother, my son and my ex-husband.

One down and five to go.

CHAPTER 24

Days of Wine and Roses

The next three Saturday nights pass exactly—and I mean exactly—the same way. Brad, Hayden, Mom and I go to the drive-in together. I fall asleep before the second feature. Brad sleeps in Hayden's bed.

And Brad and I still haven't talked about Dad.

I don't have time and it's obvious that he's reluctant to open the discussion. Because it's about Dad? Or is it about me? Who knows. He avoids being alone with me as diligently as I do with him. Because he knows I'll ask him to do something—spy on my father—that he doesn't want to do? All our meetings are tempered with company—Mom, Dad, Hayden, even T.J., who often spends the evenings with us.

I've been working long days, but I'm getting used to it again. And now that—finally—all the plates are fired, I can turn the kiln off for several days while I do the design work.

I have to turn it back on after I've designed twenty or

thirty plates, to fire them, but it's a great relief not to have to work in the overwhelming heat every day.

The slight joy I felt once I finally started the project is gone. The designs are fiddly, which would be okay if I was making only a few of them but is especially aggravating when I have three hundred and seventy-two to complete.

And I have spent the past few days—after completing six dozen last week—wondering whose idea this stupid design was in the first place. I know it was mine, but I'd thought of it as something light, fun and unique.

Any of my designs done ad infinitum would, I'm sure, cause me to have the same allergic reaction. Some days I feel as if I should break out in hives, start sneezing. I expect my eyes to turn red and tear and my body to start itching.

In fact, I wish that would happen. Then I'd have an excuse not to finish.

I'm bored and I'm cranky. And having Mr. Brad I'm-So-Perfect Mackey in the house is not making anything any bit easier.

The house is spotless. If I come in from the studio for lunch a few minutes early, I often find Brad and Hayden vacuuming or dusting or even cleaning the oven. And they're having fun at it.

Of course, when I arrive, the fun stops and the evil twin reappears.

So I'm bored, I'm cranky, I'm more than resentful of the

positive effect my ex-husband has on *my* son. Bad enough for one summer, right?

Wrong.

Because things with Dad aren't getting any better at all. I haven't been able to talk to Brad about it, but at this stage I'm not sure that would help. Almost every night we have dinner together—here, at Mom and Dad's house, at the beach, at the Way-Inn. Occasionally we go to T.J.'s and we've even been to Rowena Dale's house a couple of times.

Dad shows up one night in three. He doesn't give any excuse except to say, "I'm busy," but I can't figure out what he's busy at except that it involves the computer in the basement.

I realize that this doesn't seem all that serious—I mean, we know exactly where he is—but you have to know my father to understand how worrisome this is. My father is a man who tells you everything.

Where he's going. Why he's going. How he's going to get there and how long the trip will take. How long he's going to be there. What, precisely, he's going to do when he gets there. Who he will see when he gets there. How much money he'll spend on gas, on shopping, on food.

He'll pull out his wallet and show you the pictures he carries of Hayden—dozens of them. He'll show you photos of me as a baby, of his wedding day, of the day he retired from work.

My dad hides nothing. Not ever.

Mom's worried, though she's working hard at disguising it. She's the one making the excuses.

He's got a bit of sunstroke from mowing the lawn today.

His back is sore. He's getting ready for the winter and he restacked the woodpile this morning.

But she knows she can't use too many of the he's-got-some-ache-or-pain excuses before someone, namely me, starts to worry too obviously about him. So she has other excuses.

His friend Gil is having a rough time, so he's spending a lot of time on the phone with him.

Not exactly a lie, I guess, but I bet Dad's not talking to Gil at six o'clock when we're getting together for dinner. Gil moved back to Manchester when he retired, so it's the middle of the night there.

I don't challenge Mom on it.

Or on any of the other almost lies she's been telling on my father's behalf. It would just make everything more complicated than it already is.

But I need to know what's going on so this problem can be solved.

None of this will be easy, since I'm avoiding being alone with Brad, he's avoiding being alone with me and Mom's avoiding being alone with either of us. Not to mention Dad's avoiding being alone or in a group with any of us.

Now bad enough for one summer?

Not yet.

There are only three weeks left at the Halfmoon, and underneath everything else that's worrying me there's a low hum of sorrow that I can't ignore.

It colors everything. Or rather it taints everything.

I think I'd have been better off if one Saturday I'd arrived at the drive-in and found it closed. No warning. Or if it had been gone, demolished by some freak windstorm or torn down by greedy developers.

It's the waiting that's the hard part, waiting and not knowing what I'll do without a piece of my heart. It will leave a gap, a big one, and I don't have any idea of how to fill it.

I remember the first time I went to the drive-in without my parents.

I was already thirteen and T.J.'s thirteenth birthday was coming up—one of the advantages I have held over her for most of our lives. *I'm older than you, nyah, nyah, nyah.*

Her dad wanted to treat us for her birthday and the drive-in was the treat. T.J. and I, a couple of other friends who have long since moved on and T.J.'s dad in the driver's seat.

Looking back, I think what a brave man he was, chauffeuring four teenage girls to a double feature, voluntarily locking himself in a small metal object where the giggles and shrieks would crescendo and echo until the noise became unbearable—even to me.

But he did it because he'd do anything for T.J. I'm glad I gave her the money from the damn cat plates—it's the one thing that's gone well all summer.

That night he picked me up first, then the other girls. What I remember best are their giggles. One was high-pitched but sweet; the other as grating as a giggle could be. He had a big car, so popular in those days, but I remember thinking that it wasn't as well suited for the drive-in as my dad's station wagon. Even then I was a drive-in snob.

My dad's big old station wagon was the perfect drive-in car and T.J.'s dad had only a regular car—not as roomy, not as wide windows for watching the screen. Even worse, when we got there, he parked too far back and too far off to the side. I knew the picture would be distorted, because that's what my mother had told me dozens of times over the years when I was running late.

We need to get there early. We need to be in the middle, Aimee, otherwise we won't get a true picture. The faces will look wrong, the figures will appear odd and we won't be able to see the action properly.

That's why we always tried to arrive early, so we could get the exact right spot, the same spot every week. Mr. Miller didn't understand this, so we were doomed to a lousy space.

Mr. Miller didn't understand the necessity of quiet—or at least relative quiet—during the movie, either. T.J.

had been to the drive-in with me and my parents enough
times that she'd absorbed my mother's moviegoing rules,
but the other two girls giggled and talked and joked all
through the movie and T.J.'s dad didn't stop them.

He sat behind the wheel, his left arm resting on the
window—he hadn't even known to put the speaker on his
window so it would be in the control of a responsible adult
but had abandoned the volume control to a child.

His right wrist rested on top of the steering wheel as if
he were ready at any moment to drive away.

But he bought us anything we wanted from the concession, and this was—to me, who'd only ever had food and
drink brought from home—enough to make up for any of
his other deficiencies in movie etiquette.

We ate popcorn, of course, and red licorice and Junior
Mints. At intermission we got hot dogs and fries and later
we drank huge glasses of Pepsi and orange soda and hot
chocolate, followed by ice cream and more popcorn.

And then all four of us were sick on the trip home. T.J.'s
dad didn't complain, not even when T.J. didn't quite
manage to roll down the window before she threw up,
which, of course, set off the rest of us.

He just smiled, handed us napkins and said, "Guess this
means you all had enough to eat, huh?"

I don't remember what movies we saw, but I do recall
how that red licorice tasted—both going down and

coming up. I haven't eaten it since. And it was decades before I could eat another hot dog.

I had my next hot dog the year Hayden started pre-school. Hot dog day and it was my turn to man the mustard and ketchup. After fifty hot dogs passed by, after wiping twenty-three little chins, after smothering all those buns, I had to have one myself. It was good.

And every hot dog day since then I've had a hot dog, even the days I wasn't working the mustard and ketchup lineup.

I remember other nights at the drive-in. I remember my very first kiss—Mark James—when I wasn't quite sixteen.

I remember the night T.J. told me about Chris and why she *had* to marry him. At the time, still a teenager and quite naive, I'd thought of how much fun T.J. must be having. No longer a virgin. Pregnant. Getting married.

I remember the night I learned how wrong I was. It was winter, so the heater on my old car was running and it was noisy. So was T.J.'s baby.

Her life wasn't fun. It was hard work with no help. It was trying to make ends meet with one baby, another on the way and a husband who was allergic to work.

And I remember learning something else that night. That everyone's life wasn't like my parents' or the lives I'd seen in the brightly colored movies I'd watched as a child.

Life, or at least T.J.'s life, seemed closer to *Who's Afraid of Virginia Woolf?* than to *Gidget Goes Hawaiian*.

What else do I remember? What other nights were special enough for them to stand out among the two thousand or more Saturday nights I have spent at the Halfmoon?

Well, there's the night Brad proposed—we saw *Fanny and Alexander*. And the night I told him about Hayden—we saw *Babette's Feast*. You can tell both those events happened in the off-season because we were seeing foreign films.

I don't usually or even often remember the movies, so those two nights are exceptions. What I do remember are the people I was with.

And that's what I'll miss most of all.

CHAPTER 25

Eat Drink Man Woman

The house and studio are deserted today. Brad and Hayden have gone camping overnight and I've decided to take my first day off in a month.

The calendar in the kitchen glares at me, reminding me of all the things I want to forget.

My father hasn't been to the drive-in with us for weeks. My father hasn't been seen by me in days.

After this Saturday, there is only one more Saturday to go.

The damn cat plates have to be shipped in ten days, and I still have sixty to finish. I'm not even counting the two days it'll take to get them packed up and on the truck.

It's almost the end of summer and Brad has shown no signs of getting ready to leave. He's not packing, not looking restless, not talking—at least in my presence, and I'm willing to bet not in Hayden's, either—about a new bike or a new story.

And Hayden, when he can't see me watching him, is

lit up like a sparkler. If Brad has told him when he's leaving, there's no sign of it. Hayden treats Brad as if he'll be here forever.

But it's my day off and I'm not going to think of these things—at least not this morning. I'm going to putter around my house, which seems to have become at least as much Brad's as mine.

Mom's off to the city for the day, so I'm going over to their house after I psych myself up to it and I'm going to talk to my father.

Then, after that undoubtedly stressful meeting, I'm going to meet T.J. at the Way-Inn.

The day spreads out in front of me like an ice-cream sandwich when you don't like vanilla. You love the chocolate cookie outside, but the vanilla ruins it for you.

Okay, not such a great simile, but I'm trying to convince myself that the middle of the day won't be so bad, that my father will have a great reason for missing the drive-in and all of the dinners.

He's working on a new cabinet for Mom's collection of bowls and he doesn't want to tell her about it.

He's learning how to play the electronic keyboard he got for Christmas ten years ago.

He's working on a special gift for Hayden for going back to school. It's a handcrafted canoe.

He's started playing online poker and is addicted. Now he's trying to make back all the money he's lost.

He's selling off his collection of old tools on eBay and making a zillion dollars.

I wish.

I have no idea how my father will respond to my questions. Except for his continuing odd behaviour when I've seen him, he's been fine. Maybe a little quieter than usual, but that could be for many reasons.

This summer I've hardly seen him alone. Of course, I've been in the studio almost all of the time for the past few weeks.

I see Brad and Hayden occasionally for lunch if the three of us are in the kitchen at the same time. And I have dinner with them unless they've gone away or are out late.

They've been down to the city, arriving home with lengthy and loud stories of their adventures in amusement parks, aquariums and museums. They've done road trips up the coast to Powell River and across to Vancouver Island. One day, to Hayden's everlasting delight, they even flew over to the far west coast of Vancouver Island and spent the day in Tofino.

I envy them these trips. I envy the joy the two of them have found in each other's company. I envy the easy relationship Brad has with Hayden. And my mother. And T.J. And everyone else he runs into.

And it's not just because my good boy is slowly winning over the evil twin with the help of Brad. No, it's much worse than that.

I want to have Hayden's relationship with Brad. I want things to be back to the way they were between us when Brad and I were more than just parents, when we were friends, partners in life together. When we were lovers.

But he's shown little sign of wanting anything more from me than we have right now.

We're friends, I guess, but not close ones, at least by my measure. We don't sit and chat at the end of the day. We don't laugh at each other's jokes before the punch line is spoken. We don't…well, there are so many things we don't do I don't have the energy to list them all.

Nor do I want to. Because if I started listing them, it would simply bring home to me all the things I'm missing and all the things I want.

I need to spend some time alone with Brad. I need to know if he still wants me. And I need to know when he's leaving.

And is that a change from the past few weeks? You betcha. I've spent them avoiding Brad and now—before he starts making plans to leave—I'm trying to figure out a way to make him stay.

Bah. I'm just a seething mass of uncontrolled emotions. Envy. Lust. Sorrow. Worry.

But I've been hiding it well, locked up in the studio. No

one except T.J. has even noticed what a mess I am. Any oddities in my behavior have been dismissed as pressure because of the damn cat plates.

And that's fine with me. I definitely don't want to get into any conversation—with anyone—about all the things that are worrying me.

I putter around in the kitchen for an hour, forcing myself *not* to re-rearrange the cupboards Brad has rearranged. He's doing ninety percent of the cooking. I think all I've done in the past few weeks is burn toast and make coffee.

Now that I think about it, Brad and Hayden have done everything all summer. Cooked, cleaned, shopped. I haven't even baked, which is the one kitchen task I love.

I hear the cookie sheet calling to me.

"They deserve a treat," I say to my reflection in the oven door. Unlike the rearview-mirror woman, this reflection doesn't talk back. "And Hayden loves chocolate-chip." I don't mention Brad's name, though it's true that chocolate-chip cookies are his favorite, too.

It feels good to have my hands in cookie dough, good to be creating something other than the damn cat plates.

Three dozen cookies later, I'm just getting started.

Dad loves cinnamon twists, so I make those.

Mom's addicted to chocolate macaroons, so those are next. And easy because they don't require baking.

Apple pie for T.J. and an extra one to take to her dad. I slow my baking frenzy a bit at that thought. I haven't been to see him for weeks, but T.J. would have said something if he wasn't okay. She would, wouldn't she?

I grab the phone and dial her number, smearing sugar, butter and chocolate all over the receiver. I don't wait for her to say hello, I jump right in.

"Is your dad okay?"

"Aimee? You sound crazy. But, yes, he's fine. I saw him this morning. As always."

I sigh and try wiping off the mess without interrupting the call. It doesn't work and the receiver hits the counter with a splat. I pick it up, smearing even more baking ingredients on it. And the counter.

"Oh, T.J., I've been so busy and so distracted. I haven't seen him for weeks."

"He's fine. Really."

I'm listening carefully to see whether T.J. is angry or hurt that I haven't been to see her dad. But she sounds fine. Better than fine. She still sounds happy.

"I'll go over this afternoon. And you'll be here after work?"

"Do you want me to bring anything?"

"No, I think I've got it all under control."

I stop worrying about Mr. Miller, but I can't stop feeling that I've neglected far too much this summer.

I end the baking marathon with raspberry scones for

Rowena Dale and pack up everything—except the chocolate-chip cookies and T.J.'s apple pie—for delivery.

A shower is a must. I'm covered with bits of dough, drops of vanilla, raspberry and chocolate stains, and I swear I've got sugar coating every strand of my hair. Even my feet are dirty.

Reminder to self: never bake in your bare feet.

The tin containing the cinnamon twists is at the top of the pile of tins and plastic containers I carry out to the car.

"Time to shoulder those responsibilities," I say to the woman in the rearview mirror. "Time to talk to Dad."

CHAPTER 26

The Lawnmower Man

Mom's car is missing when I get to my parents' house—just as I'd planned it. I'm amazed because so little this summer is working out the way I thought it would. I wouldn't be surprised if Dad's not home, either, despite the fact that his once-inviolate schedule guarantees he will be.

I can't tell. The garage door is closed. There's no growling lawn mower—not that there would be: it's Friday and not Sunday or Thursday. The blinds are drawn—again, not surprising. Mom doesn't like to take the risk of her furniture fading. Or her carpets. Or her artwork.

It's stupid, but now that I'm here I'm too nervous to go up to the front door. Instead I go over to the path that runs beside the house.

I peer in each window, listening and looking. No sign of Dad.

The kitchen drapes are open, revealing a room as spotless as ever. And no evidence of my father.

I'm starting to spook myself, creeping around the house in the bright summer sun. But I continue around the back, the tin of cinnamon twists in my sweaty hands.

He must be in the basement, I think, because there's nowhere else for him to be. But of course there is. He could be in the garage, the potting shed or one of the three bathrooms in the house. He could have gone for a walk or to visit someone down the street. He could have been picked up by a friend for a game of cards, lawn bowling or pool.

He could be anywhere.

Still, I keep searching. I have a key to the house on my key ring, but I would feel uncomfortable using it under these circumstances, though neither of my parents would object. They'd expect me to use it.

But I don't.

The big garage is in the shadow of the house at this time of the day. I peer in the windows but see nothing moving.

The shelves are filled with decades of our lives: badminton, tennis and squash rackets; three or four sets of boccie balls; horseshoes; croquet balls and mallets of all different colors because we had to keep buying extra sets so that everyone who wanted could play at the same time.

There were times playing croquet in my parents' backyard when I imagined myself in Wonderland. There'd be ten or fifteen or sometimes even twenty of us, Mom presiding over it all like the Queen of Hearts, and I'd be waiting for her to say, *Off with her head*.

I cup my hands around my eyes and look harder in the garage window. My history is in this garage. And, unlike my life with Brad, the epiphanies I've had this summer haven't changed this part of my past.

I can't really see much. But I know that Dad has swept the floor, washed the windows, dusted the boxes and checked the mousetraps sometime in the past month. It's one of the things he does every month.

Okay, he's not in the garage. I wander over to the potting shed, stopping to admire my mother's dahlias and gladiolas, as well as my father's raspberries and tomatoes.

I pull a few raspberries from the canes and stuff them into my mouth.

"Aimee?"

I choke on the last berry and feel my face turn red as I try to swallow it. I cough and it explodes from my mouth like a spitball.

"You okay, love?" my father asks.

"Yes, but you scared me to death," I say, thrusting the tin of cinnamon twists into his hand. "Where were you?"

"In the potting shed, getting some string." He holds up white twine. "For the tomatoes. They're getting a bit droopy, don't you think?"

This is the father I remember and I wonder if Mom and

I have been worrying for nothing. But if so, where has he been all summer?

I turn him so that the sun is in his face. "Stand there for a minute," I say, my hands grabbing his biceps. "Just let me take a good look at you."

He complies, but he doesn't look too thrilled. His eyes—the exact shade as Hayden's—watch me carefully. I'm not sure what he expects.

I take the cinnamon twists and the twine from his hands and put them on the chair next to me and then I return my hands to his arms. I don't want him to move. Not yet.

I turn his palms up in my hands and lean close enough so I can see every line, every callus, every scar. My father's hands are as tough as he is. But there's nothing new in his palms, nothing to worry me.

His heart is next. I place my hand on his chest, bow my head and take a deep breath so I can feel the beat of it. Thump-thump. Thump-thump. Slow and even.

Okay, now I'm starting to feel pretty silly, but I've begun this and I have to finish it. I didn't plan this. Not at all. I came here to talk to him. But now I've begun, I'm going to finish it.

His checkup, as always, is the third week in November, and maybe, just maybe, that's too far away. I'm going to make sure he's healthy.

You're not a doctor, Aimee Anouk King.

The rearview-mirror woman is talking to me again.

I ignore the voice and turn my father's head side to side, checking the mobility of his neck. He gives a little squeak of discomfort when I twist it too far.

"Sorry," I say, but I don't mean it.

You didn't even pass your Red Cross CPR test.

Next his face. His eyes are clear, no red lines in them, no yellow, no sagging eyelids. His skin is slightly reddened by the sun, but there are no blotches, moles or other marks.

"Okay," I say and let him go.

He pulls away from me and sits down heavily in the chair, carefully moving the cinnamon twists first.

"What was all that about?"

I move another chair across from him and sit down, our knees practically touching. *Pull no punches*, I think.

"I'm worried about you. Mom's worried about you. Even Brad's worried about you."

He closes his eyes and then coughs, the cough he uses when he doesn't want to use words. He never wants to use the words.

"I'm not losing it. We're all worried about you. What have you been up to this summer?"

He coughs again.

"Stop it," I say. "This is serious."

His face reddens a bit and he keeps his eyes lowered. This is Dad's embarrassed look.

Knowing that whatever he's going to tell me—because he *is* going to tell me—is something he's ashamed of makes me cringe. Anything I can think of that might cause this reaction is bad, very bad.

"What is it? Why aren't you having dinner with us? Why aren't you coming to the Halfmoon? What are you doing in the basement?" I think of one more question. "And when did you learn to use the computer?"

Dad, who isn't stupid, answers the easy question first.

"I took a computer course in the spring, remember? At the library."

I don't remember. And that's T.J.'s fault. She had me working so hard catching up for the summer, all I remember is the studio and Saturday nights at the drive-in. I know I saw Mom and Dad—I see them at least two or three times a week, usually more than that—but I don't have any recollection of the computer course.

But I bet Hayden does. Because I bet Hayden helped Dad with the computer.

"Okay, so you know how to use the computer," I say. "But what are you doing with it?"

"That isn't any of your business, you know."

Dad's trying a defense he's tried many times over the years with my mother that has never yet succeeded: he's clutching at straws.

If Mom wants to know something—from me or from

Hayden or from Dad—she will get the answer. Ignore her all you want, walk away from her questions, tell her it's none of her business or you don't want to talk about it. None of these responses helps. My mother is the queen of the wearing-you-down tactic. It *always* works.

And I've learned from the best.

"It *is* my business. It's Mom's business. It's Hayden's business. We're all worried about you."

That isn't quite a lie. More like one of Mom's almost lies. Because if Hayden knew that Mom and I were worried about his grandfather, he'd be worried, too.

"You're not yourself this summer."

What if he's sick? What if he's doing research on some disease on the Internet?

I'd thought of a million reasons why he was avoiding all of us this summer, but him being sick wasn't one of them. I'll bet, though, that Mom's thought about it. That would explain the strained look on her face.

"Are you sick?"

Finally he smiles at me. "There's nothing wrong with me, Aimee. Nothing."

"I don't believe you," I say, leaning forward and putting my hands on top of his. "Something's wrong. You're not yourself."

"I am," he insists. "I just want to try something new."

CHAPTER 27

What's New, Pussycat?

Something new, something borrowed, something blue.

If my mother heard me say that, she'd laugh. When Brad and I got married, we had the ceremony on the beach. I wore orange and gold, a T-shirt and skirt I'd owned forever. I didn't borrow anything from anyone, not even my mother or T.J., and I didn't have a single blue item—not even my eyes are blue.

"What's the something new, Dad?"

I can't let myself be distracted. I've spent all summer thinking about all the things that are worrying me and avoiding dealing with my father. It's time.

"It's nothing for you to worry about."

Another time-honored King defense, and this one doesn't work any better than the first. The appropriate response is an official one.

"You can't tell me what to worry about."

This is the worst place to be having this conversation.

I smell the flowers in the garden, lush and ripe and sweet. The tomatoes are heavy and I can't help but reach over and touch the vines. There is nothing more summery than the smell of tomatoes. The apples in the gnarled tree at the back of the garden are sparkling red in the sunlight, and the raspberries are warm with the heat of the sun.

This garden is one of my favorite places in the world, especially in August.

Because by August I would start fretting about going back to school. I wasn't a scholar, not by a long shot. I liked working with my hands. I liked Home Ec, I liked Shop, I loved art class. Everything else, except bookkeeping, I just barely managed—and I got that far with a lot of help from T.J.

Dad knew how hard it was for me to go back to school, so he planned a series of adventures for me—adventures where I had to go no farther than my own backyard.

We built my very first pottery wheel right here in the garage and then I spent every day for the rest of the month with my hands in clay.

We decided to make salsa long before Mexican or Spanish food came to the Sunshine Coast. Mom had seen a recipe in one of her travel magazines and we were overrun that year with tomatoes, so Dad thought, *Why not?* We gathered tomatoes and green peppers and onions and cilantro—which wasn't easy to find on the Sunshine Coast in those days—and hot sauce and we got to work.

I can still remember the pain of that experiment. My fingers ached from chopping, burned from the hot sauce. My eyes were puffed out so much from cutting up the onions I could barely see. I was sick to death of the smell of tomatoes and green peppers.

But we made eighty jars of salsa and it was a huge hit. We even sold it at the summer fair and Dad and I became business partners. I used my half of the proceeds to buy books about pottery; Dad used his to buy more exotic tomato plants.

We never made salsa again. We never repeated any of our adventures. It was always something new, something different, and it was always only the two of us.

"Dad? It may not be anything for me to worry about, but I am worried. Please tell me."

He smiles again and pats my knee. "It's still none of your business. I'll talk to your mother about it when she gets home. Then she can tell you if she wants."

I know this is all I'm going to get from him. He'll tell Mom, and Mom might or might not tell me. I'm not any better off and won't be until I see Mom and her reaction to whatever the big secret is.

Instead of worried, now I'm angry. A very slight improvement and one I'm not sure I'm capable of appreciating.

I don't think my father has ever once denied me anything—at least anything as reasonable as this request.

He told me when I was fifteen I couldn't have a Corvette unless I could figure out a way to pay for it myself. I never did. The most splashy car I've owned has been the two-tone blue GMC pickup I bought when I finished high school, and it was almost ten years old when I got it.

He wouldn't let me go away for the weekend with Bobby MacDonald when I was in the eleventh grade. Probably a good choice, as Bobby ended up in jail that weekend for drinking and driving.

"You can't tell me?" I ask, trying one more time.

"I could tell you, of course," he says and smiles at me again. "But I'm not going to. I should tell your mother first."

And that worries me, because what if it is another woman? Or a disease?

"It's not anything bad?"

I feel like a child asking these questions, knowing that there's nothing I can do to force an answer. And if I get an answer, it's likely to be something like, *Because I said so*. Poor Hayden. He must feel like this all the time.

"It's not bad," Dad says. "Everything's going to be okay."

He stands up and reaches down to hug me. I burrow into the warmth of his shirt and the smell of him, so familiar and so safe. He tolerates that for a few moments and then pushes me away.

"Now," he says. "What's up with you?"

I should have known he'd do that. Dad's a master at

turning the tables. I come to ask him questions, to get answers, and now he's questioning me.

"I made you some cinnamon twists." I grab the tin and open it, hoping to distract him.

It works but only because he allows it to. "Come on inside. I've got iced tea in the fridge that'll go perfectly with these."

My reprieve doesn't last long.

He sets the table with glasses and plates and napkins. He adds a bowl of fresh mint from the fridge and the ice-cube tray from the freezer.

"There." He sits down across from me. "Now. Tell me what you're up to."

When we sit down, he makes sure I'm in the chair opposite the window—his usual spot—and now he takes a close look at me. I know I look tired; I've been working hard. And I probably look strained, as well. Hayden and Brad and my ongoing concern with my father, not to mention the drive-in. I can't be looking my best.

"You look tired, sweetheart. Is everything okay?"

Talk about a complete about-face. Not fair, not fair at all.

"Everything's fine, Dad. I'm just tired."

"The damn cat plates?"

"Partly. But they're almost done and I'll get them shipped and delivered in time."

"How's it going with Brad and Hayden?"

"They're having a great summer."

"I didn't mean between them, I meant with you. How are you coping?"

"I'm not."

I slap my hands over my mouth. I can't believe I've just said that, and to my dad of all people. I must be losing my mind.

"It's just…it's hard, you know? Hayden loves Brad so much and he's always so happy with him, smiling and laughing. And with me he's still the evil twin."

Dad pours me some more iced tea, but he doesn't say anything, just waits for me to continue.

"I spend all day in the studio working and they go out and play. I want to go with them. But by the time I'm finished with the damn cat plates, Brad will be leaving and I won't have…"

I can't finish the sentence.

"You don't want him to leave, do you?"

"I don't know."

And I really don't know. I don't know whether I want him to stay or go. What I do know is that I want to make love with him, many times—in my bed, in his, on the beach, in the car. I want to see him looking at me the way he used to, the way that always made me feel both safe and thrilled at the same time.

Safe because I knew he'd never hurt me, thrilled

because the emotions were so volatile, so sharp and clear and almost unbearably hot.

And with Brad, the film noir me won every single time until the last. I chose the slight edge of fear, the sense of jumping off a cliff without being sure that someone would be there to catch me.

"You need to decide, Aimee. Because Brad won't wait forever."

"He's not waiting at all."

The Elvis twist of Dad's lip says it all. It says, *You're not paying attention.* It says, *Where have you been all summer?* It says, *He's waiting for you to decide what you want.* And it says, *He's not going to wait forever.*

"Oh," is what I say. It's the only word I'm capable of. "Oh," I repeat as I try to get the blood to move through my suddenly constricted heart. And "Oh," I say one more time as my lungs start working again, pushing breath in and out.

"Oh, yes," Dad says.

"But they're away today."

"Tomorrow, then. Gives you twenty-four hours to think about what you're going to do about this."

"I have to go to Rowena's," is what I say. "I made her some scones."

Dad pulls me from the chair and pushes me toward the front door. "Off you go." He opens the door and stands on the front steps, as he has for so many years, watching me walk down the sidewalk to my car. "Don't forget," he says, "neither your mom nor I are going to be at the drive-in tomorrow night."

I look back to tell him that I can't forget something I didn't know, but he's gone. Back into the house. Down into the basement. On to the computer.

But I'm not worrying about him anymore. I've got a much bigger problem.

CHAPTER 28

Something's Got to Give

Rowena lives in Gibsons, which means a drive down the peninsula to its very tip, but I don't have anything else to do and I need the distraction. Driving the Sunshine Coast Highway to Gibsons almost always manages to do that for me.

There's plenty to look at. On the left is the ocean peeking out from behind the trees and houses and resorts, the sailboats and cruisers and gillnetters white against the brilliant blue water, the red cedar roofs of the houses nestled among the rocky outcroppings.

On the right, hills rise up to join the Coast Range towering thousands of feet above the water, snow still dusting some of the peaks even in late August. Small farms, surrounded by water and mountains, make use of every half acre, stocked with cows, pigs, chickens, goats, llamas and sheep. These farms produce every kind of cheese you can imagine, every variety of eggs you could possibly want. We aren't quite self-sufficient, but I bet we're a whole lot closer to it than a lot of other communities.

We eat fish caught right off the coast, buy beef and pork direct from the farmer, eat cheese locally made. Not to mention the fruit and vegetables that grow in almost every yard and on every farm. Plates, mugs and bowls are hand-crafted by a potter who lives up the mountain or, in my case, right down the street.

I think about all of this on my way to Gibsons, slowed by the convoy of RVs and trucks hauling boats, heading to the mainland from Earls Cove. I adjust my speed as the tourists sightsee from one end of the peninsula to the other.

None of these vehicles seems to be in a hurry. These travelers aren't worried about making the ferry at Gibsons, so I'm not, either. I've got plenty of time and I occupy myself—as I used to with my father and I now do with Hayden—checking out license plates.

People show up on the Sunshine Coast from every-where. From the Maritimes and from Florida—which has to be as far away as you can get on this continent—from Maine, Louisiana, Texas and California. They come from the prairies, the mountains, the northern plains, the southern coasts, even distant Canadian provinces.

From June to September, the Sunshine Coast turns into a microcosm of North America. Last summer Hayden and I collected license plates from forty-seven states and every single province and territory in Canada. That was my best year ever.

I focus on everything and anything except Brad.

"I hope Rowena is home," I say to the woman in the rearview mirror. "Brad still has my cell phone, so I can't call her. If she's not home, I'll just leave the scones at the door."

The woman in the rearview mirror tut-tuts at me.

Remember what I told you about epiphanies? You can't ignore them.

"I'm not ignoring this one. And I'm not sure it's an epiphany. I think it's just Dad blowing steam. There's no way that Brad's waiting for me to ask to him to stay."

No?

She disappears with that comment and I continue, as best I can, to pretend that I didn't hear anything she said. I manage pretty well, too.

Rowena's house is one of the prettiest in Gibsons, and that's saying a lot. She lives high above the town on a rocky hill to the west, up, up and up. Her house is glass and cedar, with every window facing the water. The back of the house is built into the rock, and the house runs up from the water to halfway up the slope. The rooms are all terraced, directly over each other, with floor-to-ceiling windows and a balcony or patio suspended over the water.

It's no wonder that Rowena Dale looks twenty years younger than eighty. She must climb dozens and dozens of steps a day. I park the car at the top of the hill and gingerly make my way down the steep access to her front door.

And this is only the beginning. It takes a few minutes for Rowena to make it up the inside stairs to the front door, but she's talking to me already through the intercom, always an entertaining part of a visit to Rowena's.

"Who's there?"

"It's Aimee. I've brought you some raspberry scones."

"Just hold on, girl, I'm on my way."

"Where are you?" I ask, so I can decide whether to sit down on the bench and wait or lean up against the railing. If she's at the dock, I'm sitting down.

"I'm in the kitchen," she says and I lean against the railing. No need to get too comfortable: the kitchen's only three levels down, not so far in this house. Or for Rowena.

"What's up with you?" she asks. She has intercom speakers built in every few steps so she doesn't get bored coming up to answer the door.

"Not much," I say. "But I spent the morning baking—"

She doesn't let me finish my sentence. "You wanted a break from the damn cat plates? And the boys are out of town, aren't they? Must feel good to have your house back."

I nod and then remember she can't see me. "That's it."

The door flings open and there's Rowena, not a drop of sweat on her face, not a bit winded or a hair out of place. I'm amazed, as always, by her stamina.

"Come in, come in." She pulls me after her. "It's just time to have a glass of wine and a raspberry scone on the patio."

I follow her even though I had planned to drop the scones and run, because Rowena Dale is an irresistible force, a woman who will not accept no as an answer. Which must make for an odd and kind of creepy dichotomy in her life, because Rowena has said yes to marriage proposals twenty-seven times and then quickly converted all of those acceptances to rejections.

Maybe this is exactly where I need to be, maybe Rowena is the person who can make everything clear to me. Although maybe not. Rowena is a man's woman—she loves men in the way that I love throwing pots. All men. Every age, every shape, every way. But she may be my best hope.

The kitchen patio is shaded by hundred-foot cedar trees, allowing a delicate tracery of light to decorate the hardwood floors and sparkle off the glass walls and doors. Keats Island adds a touch of interest to the shining water view, and I relax into Rowena's care. I hear her puttering in the kitchen, singing Dean Martin at the top of her lungs. She loves him more than any other singer, and I sometimes wonder if he's the man she's been looking for all her life.

I have spent more time this summer, more time than I have in my life, being cared for. Brad has cooked and cleaned for me, Mom and T.J. have worried over me and the entire community—Rose, Mercedes, Doris and

Rowena, all of Mom's friends, everyone I run into on the street—has been concerned about me and the damn cat plates.

This is one of the reasons I love Halfmoon Bay. And the Sunshine Coast.

Rowena brings out a full ice bucket, with a foiled neck sticking out. I reach for the bottle, but she slaps my hand away. "My house. I get to uncork the wine. Wait."

She goes in and out a few times. Champagne flutes made by a glassblower in Secret Cove. Linen napkins. Then plates, knives, a bowl of creamy yellow butter I know she's bought from Hal's farm down the road. Finally one of my favorite platters—deep blue, the color of the ocean after the sun has set but before it's released all its light to the dark—and the raspberry scones.

"I thought champagne appropriate," Rowena says.

"Oh, good," I say and wait for her to explain. She always does.

She wraps one of the linen napkins around the neck of the bottle and tugs lightly, and the cork pops with barely a sound. Rowena is an expert at many things.

She pours peach-colored wine into both our glasses, hands me a plate and a knife and then sits back in her chair with a sigh of contentment.

"Now…" She grins as she sips her champagne. "All we need are men."

I laugh. "No. That's exactly what we don't need."

"I forgot." She waggles her eyebrows at me. "You've got Brad. And Hayden. More than enough male influence in one house."

"Right now I don't have either of them."

All of Rowena's emotions are flagged through her eyebrows. This time she raises both of them. "You don't? That's not what I'm hearing."

I don't even have to ask her from whom: I know. Mom and the gossip queens. Mom told Doris and Doris told the other queens. And one of them—probably Doris—told Rowena. Damn. There are times when the Sunshine Coast is just *too* small.

But I didn't think Mom knew, not really. I haven't caught her watching me watching Brad, haven't had a single wink from her when Brad pulls a chair from the table and waits for me to settle into it before he pushes it back in and then—why haven't I noticed this before?—sits down beside me.

But I'm not surprised. Nothing could surprise me this summer. I've spent months discovering all sorts of things that I should have already known. This is just another one of them.

Rowena's left eyebrow twitches. "Why's Brad still here? Did he lose his job?"

"Brad can't lose his job—he doesn't have one. He works

for himself, freelances for magazines, waits for someone to e-mail and ask him to restore a bike."

Just like me. I don't have a job, not a nine-to-five one, anyway. But I get by. And sometimes, like this summer, I more than get by. And so does Brad.

"So what's he doing? I see him and Hayden almost every day, collecting shells on the beach, on Mercedes's dock with fishing poles, waiting in the ferry lineup, scrambling up the trail in some park or another."

I don't know what he's doing. But Dad has put some ideas into my mind and they shoot right out of my mouth.

"Dad says he's waiting for me to make up my mind."

Both eyebrows meet in the middle for a moment and then flash back up. Rowena pours some more champagne into our glasses, obviously taking some time to think about what I've said.

I can't decide whether she's precisely the right person to talk to about Brad or the absolutely wrong one. She's got lots of experience with men, but she's been engaged twenty-seven times and she's still single.

Yeah, the rearview-mirror woman says from the shiny silver ice bucket, *but she keeps on trying. She doesn't give up. She believes in love.*

The subtext in that sentence is clear. "But maybe he doesn't want me. Maybe Dad's wrong."

Oops, I've said that out loud. The rearview-mirror

woman is laughing her fool head off, and Rowena's eyebrows meet again before she answers the question I haven't asked.

"This isn't about Brad, you know. This is about you. You were the one who told him to leave. You were the one who wouldn't take the risk of trying something new."

"But…"

But I thought I was doing the right thing.

"But nothing. He's back. He's been here all summer supporting you."

"He's been here all summer playing with Hayden."

"And cooking. And cleaning. And shopping and doing the laundry. And keeping Hayden and everyone else out of your hair so you could finish the damn cat plates."

"But…"

I don't know why it is I feel I have to question Brad's motives. It doesn't really matter why he's doing the things he's doing. I owe him a thank-you at least. Because Rowena's right. He's the only reason I've made it through the summer.

I reach for the butter and a scone. Rowena's eyebrows are somewhere up under her hairline, waiting for my answer. Only I don't know what to say.

I carefully slice the scone in half, slide a thick layer of butter on both halves and then alternate, one bite of scone, one sip of champagne, until my glass is empty and the scone is gone.

"Here," Rowena says, her eyebrows back where they

belong. "Have some more champagne. And then you need a nap before you drive again. I'm going to do the same."

She points at the blue-and-white-striped lounger at the far end of the kitchen patio. "Use that," she says. "I always sleep well there in the afternoon."

She disappears into the kitchen with the clutter from the table, then pops back out with a soft white throw. "You might need this."

CHAPTER 29

A Midsummer Night's Dream

There is something about Rowena's patio that quickly drags me from fretting to sleeping. The cedar boughs quivering with the slight breeze, the faint hush-hush of the waves on the dock below me, the warmth of the afternoon sun diluted by the shadows cast by the trees.

One minute I'm in the lounger, my eyes at half-mast, watching the boats on the water. The next I'm sound asleep.

I know this because the ocean's gone, as are the breeze and the sunshine. I'm in Dad's old station wagon at the Halfmoon. Rain patters on the windows and turns the picture on the screen from a sunny day in Italy to a rain-soaked evening.

It's a movie I've never seen before. I don't recognize anything about it. The actors are strangers, which even in the dream I find odd. The language is English, but the words have somehow twisted themselves around in the actors' mouths and I can't decipher them.

It is a room full of actors I don't know, speaking a language I know but can't understand. Definitely a dream, verging on a nightmare.

I turn my head to see who's in the car with me. I'm not surprised to see Brad. He doesn't turn on the windshield wipers so I can see the movie more clearly, and I can't really figure out why I don't ask him to do this simple thing. He just sits in the driver's seat.

It's warm and I want to take off the sweater I'm wearing, but I don't have a T-shirt under it, so I don't.

You know how dreams are? How nothing that happens in them surprises you?

I'm not surprised that I don't have on a T-shirt or bra or panties under my cotton skirt. Because it makes sense. This is how I used to dress when Brad and I went to the Halfmoon alone before Hayden.

So now I know what's happening. I know why he hasn't turned on the windshield wipers—so no one can see into the car—and why we're here by ourselves.

Even more amazingly, because this is the first time all summer I've *known* just about anything, I know why I'm having this dream.

So I also know that I can tear myself out of this dream, but I don't. I choose to stay here at the Halfmoon with my ex-husband.

Brad still isn't looking at me and I know that he's waiting for me to make the first move.

And in the dream I do.

I move across the bench seat until my thigh touches his. I take his right arm from the back of the seat and pull it around me, tugging it lower and lower until it touches my breast. Then I unbutton my sweater and place his warm, callused hand on my breast—nothing between us, skin to skin.

And then I sigh. Because it feels so good, as if I've been waiting for this for years. And I have. Even in my dream I know that this is exactly what I've been waiting for.

I'm still not convinced—despite Dad and Rowena—that this is what Brad's waiting for, but in the dream I don't care. I just carry on.

I rub my hand along his thigh, mimicking the circles he's making on my nipple. He, like me, is having trouble breathing, having trouble staying still. But he doesn't move. Neither do I. We've done this before, made love in this car, in this drive-in, and we know what to do, how to disguise our passion from any passersby.

Not that there are many. Unlike on a regular Saturday night, Brad and I are parked in Lover's Lane—the back row of the drive-in, where no one can come up behind us. And we're parked as far to the left as possible, where no one will need to pass us to get to the concession.

It's raining, but that just makes us feel safer, more hidden. And now the windows are fogging up.

I trail my hand up his thigh until I touch his erection through the denim. He shifts in the seat just a little, and I continue my circles while he presses harder into my hand.

Breathe, I tell myself. *Remember to breathe*.

That simple instruction is almost impossible to follow when Brad takes his left hand off the steering wheel and raises my skirt to my knees. I repay him by undoing the button on his jeans and then ever so slowly, ever so carefully, undoing the zipper.

He doesn't wear anything under his jeans—ever.

He strains into my hand, heat scorching my palm. And I follow his lead, sliding down in the seat until I meet his hand, until he touches me where I need to be touched.

We're careful to move slowly, to allow ourselves to savor the slow, stately dance we're creating in this car on this rain-soaked night.

He touches me and I touch him, our hands caressing, our bodies trembling just on the edge of release. This is where we want to be, right here, at this place, before the explosion, before the end, and we've learned how to stay here.

We've learned to move slowly, to touch gently, to pull back when we're too close, to wait until we can't wait any longer.

And when we can't wait any longer, he turns to me for the first kiss, the one that ignites the fire we've been tending.

"Oh," I whisper in my dream.

"Oh, my God," I whisper, my body quivering and spent on Rowena's kitchen patio, on her blue-and-white lounger. "Oh, my God."

CHAPTER 30

Tequila Sunrise

Embarrassed? Shaken? Dazed?

All of the above.

But embarrassed more than anything else. Especially waking up to find my skirt tucked up around my hips and my right hand between my legs. And a white throw placed carefully over me. The white throw I'd left at the bottom of the lounger.

Rowena has left me a note pinned to the throw.

I'm off to the Way-Inn. Just close the sliding door behind you and lock it. The front door locks by itself. Good luck with Brad. And don't do anything I wouldn't.

I picture her left eyebrow waggling as she wrote the last sentence and I laugh, fold up the white throw and take it into the kitchen with me.

When I get in the car, I head back up Highway 101, back to Halfmoon Bay to visit T.J.'s dad and drop off his apple pie.

This visit is simple. No stress, no complication, no problems, just a nice sit-down, an equally nice cup of tea with cream and sugar, a small slice of apple pie. And one of the best conversations I've had with Mr. Miller in months.

I wonder if T.J.'s noticed the improvement. Or whether, because she's seen him every day, he seems just the same to her as ever.

I'll find out—I check my watch—in a couple of hours. The house is still quiet when I get there, though the kitchen looks as if a bomb hit it. Damn. I should have cleaned up before I left, because scraping the pastry and sugar, flour, chocolate and butter off the floor, counters and stove is going to be hell now that everything has hardened.

I'd have raised a stink if Brad or Hayden left *my* kitchen like this. I'm glad Brad's not here to see what I've done to his. Because this kitchen is his—at least it has been this summer—and I will respect that.

No, really, I will. Today has forced me to turn over a new leaf. And thinking that, I run upstairs to check my wardrobe. I need to make sure I have something special to wear to the Halfmoon tomorrow night. And it has to be a skirt. And a shirt with buttons down the front.

I shiver a little as I paw through my closet and drawers. I know nothing can happen tomorrow night—Hayden will be with us—but it's the memory of that dream that's making me tremble.

Add that to the *real* memories of the *real* thing and I'm surprised I can walk at all.

The skirt and silk sweater I put on the bed are Brad's favorite colors on me. Salmon and brown and gold. I touch the sweater, loving the cool slide of the fabric beneath my fingers.

"Enough," I say. "Go clean up the kitchen."

The rearview-mirror woman appears for just a moment in the small gilded mirror above my dresser. *Take a deep breath*, she says, an evil grin lighting her face. *And don't forget to take a cold shower before Brad and Hayden get home tomorrow.* She giggles, nonchalantly waves a hand and disappears.

Sheesh, that woman is starting to drive me crazy. Oh, wait. Maybe she already has. Just seeing her and talking to her probably means I *am* crazy. So what would a crazy woman do at this juncture?

This crazy woman takes a deep breath, grabs an apron from the clean laundry pile and starts scrubbing her incredibly messy kitchen.

The chicken's marinating, the wine is chilling, the limes are sliced for margaritas. The salad is made, just waiting for the dressing, and the candles are ready to light on the patio.

I've loaded the CD player with background music, though T.J.'s likely to change it the minute she walks in.

She doesn't believe in background music, hates elevator tunes, and if she can't sing along to it, it's gotta go.

I've strategically placed all her favorite tunes next to the player so it won't take too long—I've known her to take fifteen minutes to decide what one song to play on the jukebox at the Way-Inn.

The click-click of T.J.'s heels warns me she's on the way, that she's hurrying along the sidewalk around the side of the house.

"Come on in," I yell before she gets to the patio. "I'm just finishing up in here." I swipe the hair out of my eyes and take a quick look around. Clean. No sign of the tornado that swept through this morning.

Blender and glasses at the ready, limes in a big bowl next to it, a perfectly sized shallow bowl—my own design, black with a plethora of brilliantly colored limes filling its curves—filled with salt. Tequila, Triple Sec, lime juice.

I remembered to take the bag of ice out to the patio and hammer it into smaller pieces before putting it into the ice bucket. We're ready.

T.J., of course, is wearing a black suit and panty hose, a sunset-orange shirt and black pumps.

She doesn't give me a chance to say anything before holding up a bag. "I'll be right back. I brought stuff to change into. Oh—" she turns back before closing the door to the guest bathroom "—I brought back your shorts and

T-shirt, too." The door closes and she yells from behind it, "Get that blender going, will you?"

I measure out the alcohol, the ice and the lime juice and put all of it into the blender. I plug my ears while it does its thing, fill the glasses and step outside to the patio, T.J. padding behind me with nacho chips and salsa she's taken from her bag. ·

"Okay," T.J. says, settling herself into her favorite chair, her feet up on the bench Hayden and Brad made last week. "Spill."

There's no point in asking her what or how she knows there's something *to* spill or where she heard about it. None of those things matter. Sometimes T.J. just knows, and this might be one of those times.

But I'm willing to bet my new-this-spring wheel—the one I'd been lusting after for years—that Rowena Dale and T.J. had a little conversation sometime this afternoon. And I'm willing to bet every last one of the damn cat plates that before Rowena called T.J., she'd already talked to my father.

Who, I'm willing to bet Hayden's best bike, has already told my mother all about everything. And that reminds me—I need to call her. Now.

"T.J.? I'll spill in a minute, but I have to check on something with my mom. If I can borrow your cell, I don't have to go inside and you can hear it at the same time as I do."

She pulls the cell from the pocket of her shorts and hands it to me. I'm shaking and she's lying back in that chair as if she hasn't a care in the world. I want to be her just for a moment. I want to stop worrying about everything.

I want my father *not* to be crazy. I want Brad to want me. And I want the drive-in to stay open forever. I figure I might end up—if I'm very very lucky—with two out of three. And as Meat Loaf says, two outta three ain't bad.

"Mom? You at home?"

I pass the cell to T.J., whispering, "Put it on speaker, okay?"

"Mom," I speak a little louder, "T.J.'s with me and we can both hear you, okay?"

"What are you two up to?"

She's put her hand over the handset, but I hear her yelling at Dad. "It's Aimee and T.J. I'll be a few minutes, so don't put on the salmon yet." She doesn't trust Dad with fish. Burgers, steaks—okay, they can be burned. But over-cooked salmon? No way.

"What? What?" She's still yelling. "Of course I'm going to tell them. Why do you think she phoned?"

T.J. and I both giggle.

"You're drinking, aren't you?" Mom asks.

"Sort of," T.J. says. "I've had one sip of the margarita in my hand."

"Aimee?" Mom asks.

"Hmm. I had champagne with Rowena at lunchtime but nothing since. I haven't even had a taste of my margarita yet. But tell us, will you? The suspense is killing me."

"Tell you what?"

This is Mom at her worst. She knows what I want her to tell me, but she's going to make me beg for it.

"You know, about Dad. He told me this morning that he'd tell you first and then you could tell me."

"And me," T.J. pops in. "Tell me, too."

"Your father is working on getting his degree."

"He's what?" T.J.'s voice and mine squeal into phone in unison.

"He's started on a bachelor's degree at the University of Northern British Columbia. In English literature."

I'm hoping that my face doesn't look quite as shocked as T.J.'s, but the way she's staring back at me, I know that it must. My father? A degree? *In English?* The sky is falling.

"Mom? You're not kidding?"

"Of course not. He showed me the course materials. And we're going down to the city tomorrow so he can buy all the books he needs. Bye now. We have to have dinner and then we have to pack."

I'm so shocked I don't know what to say. But, as always, she does.

"The keys to the station wagon are on the front hall table. See you Monday."

Even with the risk of another brain-freeze headache I do it, I gulp down the margarita. And then I pour another from the pitcher sitting in the ice bucket on the table. I gulp down half of that one before I can speak.

"I don't know if my dad's ever read a whole book in his life. An *English* degree?"

T.J. reaches over for the pitcher. "Great, isn't it?"

I nod and pour the rest of this batch of margaritas into my glass.

Yeah, I think, *it's great*. My father isn't going crazy. My best friend isn't fooling around on her soon-to-be-ex husband. As for Hayden—if T.J. says he'll grow out of it, grow out of it he will. The damn cat plates are almost finished.

What I don't understand is why I'm left with the complicated problems. Why couldn't I—or someone else—have solved the big problems? The Brad problem. The Halfmoon Drive-In problem.

I have two weeks to solve the drive-in problem and heaven knows how long to solve the Brad problem. I'd better get with it.

CHAPTER 31

The Big Easy

This Saturday and one more. This night and then one more next week. And then it's over.

Hayden will go back to school on Tuesday—Labor Day is early this year—leaving me alone in the house with Brad. The damn cat plates will be done on Wednesday and shipped on Friday. Leaving me without an excuse to spend all day hiding from Brad in the studio.

And what will Brad do once Hayden goes back to school? He hasn't shown any signs of planning his departure, hasn't made any long-distance calls on the house phone or my cell. I haven't seen him drooling over any bikes, buying travel or bike magazines or watching chopper or travel shows.

If I didn't know anything about him, about his relationship to this place, I would think he's settled right in. Permanently.

And that's the question I'm not ready to ask him. Not

yet. Not until I know if he really is waiting for me to ask him to stay.

The question I am ready to ask is complicated by the presence of our son. But my mother, bless her psychic little heart, solves it for me.

I've been in the studio since six, trying to take advantage of the cooler mornings now that August is almost over. Today I've plugged the CD player with crying songs—Patsy Cline, Chet Baker, Billie Holiday, Leonard Cohen. I don't know why exactly, because they're not making me cry. Maybe it's because they're the kind of songs I can sing along to, that center me, hold me in place, because all my life I've listened, danced and sung along with them, with T.J. and Rose and my mother.

And, boy, do I need that. I'm shaking in my boots because I want to ask my ex-husband if he's interested in sleeping with me. But if he says yes, that's only the first step. Then there's the I-made-a-mistake step, followed by the are-you-interested-in-trying-again? step.

If he says yes again, that's followed by the what-do-we-do-next? step, the telling-the-parents-T.J.-and-Hayden step, the oh-my-God-I'm-not-ready-to-do-this-again step.

I can't help it, I'm making myself crazy here. But at least the damn cat plates are going well and I don't have a hangover. T.J. and I stopped with the first batch of margaritas.

"Your dad? An English degree? Can you imagine him reading Virginia Woolf?" T.J. had asked.

"Or Dickens or Chaucer? It'll take him a year to read one of those books," I'd replied.

We'd adjourned to the library, pawed through the paperbacks on the bottom shelves, the ones left over from high school and college, the ones I buy because I hear on a TV or radio show that they're supposed to be one of the best books of the century. And I read them, I force myself to read them. I've read them all.

But I can't imagine my father reading any of them. He does read—newspapers and magazines, and murder mysteries. So maybe it's not so odd to think about Dad going to college, getting an English degree. Maybe it makes an odd kind of sense, and at least he's not in some Internet chat room.

When T.J. went home, I went to bed. But, of course, I didn't sleep. I haven't slept much this summer.

I'm down to the last thirty plates and I've got three days—I have to go to school with Hayden on Tuesday—to finish them.

This laying out of my future is something I've done all my life, something I can't stop myself from doing. When I decided I wanted to be a potter, I paced off my entire possible future and then started on the path to follow it.

A few craft fairs, maybe a store or two.

Rent a studio with a kiln a couple of days a week.

Buy books and magazines and study, study, study.

Build up an inventory.

Take some great photos and start shopping the work around.

More craft fairs—the really good, expensive ones.

A few more stores, some permanent inventory.

Rent a studio full-time.

Buy my own kiln.

The list went on right up to the Governor General's Award I'd win for visual arts, the Order of Canada, the obituary I'd get in the potters' guild magazine, the funeral.

Of course, because I was preparing for a particular kind of future, there was no Brad, no Hayden. No house or studio of my own. Definitely no damn cat plates.

And here I am doing it again. Planning it out step by step by step. Seduce Brad. Then the next step. And after that the next step.

But it won't work the way I've planned it, never has, never will.

The woman in the rearview mirror is laughing at me even though I can't see her—not too many reflective surfaces in the studio.

Back to my mother's psychic heart. It's not even nine o'clock and there's someone in running shoes racing around the house to the backyard, toward the studio.

"Mom. Mom." It's Hayden and he's calling me. I hug myself for a minute, straighten my face out of its joyous expression—I don't want to scare him—and yell, "Come in."

"Grandma and Grandpa are going to Vancouver and they want me to go with them. We can go to the Pacific National Exhibition, Mom."

My mother is standing by the door, her face turned toward the shelves piled with the damn cat plates as if she doesn't want me to see her expression. I hear Brad and my father on the patio, unloading the bags from the Mustang and waiting for my consent—I assume they're waiting for my consent—before transferring some of Hayden's gear to Dad's car.

I will my mother to turn her face toward me, and she does, though she's hiding whatever it is she's thinking about. Her face is calm, a slight smile—a cat's smile—tugging at her lips.

I know what it is she's thinking because I'm thinking exactly the same thing. I know she's talked to Rowena Dale and Dad and they've told her the conversations they had with me yesterday. And I know that sometime last night, after T.J. and I talked to her on the phone, she and my dad—and maybe Rowena—concocted this scheme.

Well, she's not going to get away with it.

"Is Brad going with you?" I ask, my face innocent and my voice cheerful.

She grins at the question and shakes her head. "This is

just for Hayden. And there won't be room in the car for all of us once your dad picks up all the books he needs.

"Besides, Hayden will keep me company—" she ruffles his hair and gives him a quick hug "—while Bill spends hours in the bookstore."

Hayden smiles back at her and then returns to me. He's careful not to touch anything as he passes through the studio, not to jostle the plates or get too near the kiln. He's still smiling, and even though I've told myself not to, I smile right back at him.

I set the plate I'm painting on the table and look across at him. He smiles at me again and then reaches around my waist for a hug.

When I look across the room at my mother, the tears in her eyes match the ones I feel in mine. I blink to dislodge them and hug Hayden back, not too hard, and say, "You can go, but you make sure you're back here early tomorrow. You need to start getting ready for school on Tuesday. And I'll bet you any money we have to go shopping."

CHAPTER 32

Sleeping Beauty

The three boys—my father, my son and my ex-husband—pile Hayden's bags in the car. Mom and I watch from the sidewalk.

"Come on, come on. Let's get going. We won't make the eleven-o'clock ferry if we don't leave right now." Mom chases Dad and Hayden into the car as if she were shooing chickens back into the henhouse.

I stand on the sidewalk and watch as the car reaches the end of the road and disappears around the corner. I've already calculated the hours between now and their return—exactly thirty of them—when Brad and I will be alone in the house.

Maybe alone in the station wagon at the drive-in. My face heats at the memory of my dream and I shake my head, trying to shake the memory of the dream and the memory of the real thing right out of my head so I can make it through the next thirty hours without making a complete fool of myself.

I don't know whether that's possible, but I'm going to give it a shot.

Brad hasn't moved since the car doors slammed, leaving the two of us standing on the sidewalk in the August sun. Neither have I.

One of us has to blink first.

It's me. "I have to get back to the studio," I say, my back to him. "I only have a few days and I have thirty plates left. It's good that Hayden's away—I can work right into the evening and not have to worry about the drive-in."

I hear a slight growl from Brad. "Oh, we're still going to the drive-in, babe," he says. "There are only two more weeks left and I'm not going to miss one of them."

"You can go without me. Call T.J. or Rowena." I hesitate. "You must know someone who'll go with you."

"I do. And that someone is you."

He grabs my arm and manhandles me around the house to the door of the studio. "Now get in there." He shoves open the door and me inside, but he doesn't close it behind me. Not yet. "I'll go over and pick up the station wagon. Seven o'clock. Be ready."

He starts to close the door and then stops again. "I'll leave sandwiches in the fridge for lunch. I have some things I need to do this afternoon."

This time he closes the door and I scurry over to the table and pick up a plate. And then put it right back down. My hands are shaking too much to be able to paint a single line.

I turn the CD player back on and sit in the spinning chair, taking deep breaths one after another until I feel my body relax into the seat. I hold my hands in front of me. They're still shaking.

More deep breaths, a little humming along to "My Funny Valentine" and I try again. They're still trembling but this time I have to look carefully to see them move.

A glass of water, a couple of waltzes around the room to "Crazy"—how appropriate—and I sit back down in the spinning chair to check again. This time my hands have stopped trembling, and I go back to work. I have to finish at least ten plates today—fifteen would be better, leave me with less pressure when Hayden gets back tomorrow afternoon.

By the time my stomach is growling so loudly I can't resist, I've finished twelve plates. And I'm starving. I check in the driveway for the Mustang. It's gone.

The sandwiches are on a plate on the counter—egg salad on brown, not too much mayo, radishes and red peppers in the filling. Just like the ones Sam makes for me, just like the ones I used to make for Brad.

I don't take any chances. I take the plate, a Diet Pepsi and a peach from the tree in the garden and hurry back to the studio. Leonard Cohen is singing "I'm Your Man" as I sit down on the spinning chair and put my feet up on the table.

I've spent the morning focused on the plates and the music. Now I'm planning: the painful hours and hours of packing the plates so they don't crack or break, the shipping, Hayden's back-to-school shopping, the next few weeks. Anything but think about this night. And Brad. And the Halfmoon.

And I've succeeded pretty well. I bet I only got distracted every sixty seconds or so. Really. And I do have a plan for everything—except the next few weeks.

That's Brad's fault.

But I don't care. He can stay forever if he wants. That first hug from Hayden? That one tiny hug is worth all the aggravation that might flow from Brad's presence in this house.

I don't have a clock in the studio and I didn't put on my watch this morning. It's August, so I know almost exactly what time it is by the rays from the sun on the wall. Right now the light is about halfway between the middle two shelves so that means it's about five o'clock.

And I'd better get moving if I want to have time for a nap and a shower before seven. I pull the drapes in my bedroom but leave the window open to the breeze, which brings the aroma of roses, day lilies and peonies into the room. I close my eyes and watch the red light on my eyelids fade to black, picturing the sunset on the beach.

The soft cotton sheets caress my skin and I snuggle in a little deeper, twisting the sheets around my tired body. *Lie still, Aimee. Relax.* The voice comes from the mirror above my dresser, and for the first time this summer I find myself agreeing with the rearview-mirror woman.

I need to sleep. I need to stop the anticipation that's thrumming through my veins. I need to get Brad's face off the back of my eyelids.

I've not slept much this summer, making do with short naps in the afternoons and long, fretting nights of inter-rupted slumber. I know my eyes are framed by dark shadows, but there's been nothing I can do about it.

So I lie back into the bed, keep my eyes closed and relax—my feet, calves, thighs, arms, shoulders and neck, the muscles in my jaw and forehead.

Eventually I drop, not into sleep but into calm. And that seems to be enough.

When I hear the familiar sound of the station wagon pulling into the driveway, I'm relaxed enough to remember to make my bed, to clean the shower behind me. I'm not relaxed enough to remember to leave off my panties and bra.

That, I have to be reminded about. And it's one more reason to thank the woman in the rearview mirror.

CHAPTER 33

Wings of Desire

He's not in the kitchen when I reach the bottom of the stairs, nor is he on the patio waiting for me. But something else is.

Roses. Dozens and dozens of roses—from my garden, from my mother's garden, from the nursery at Pender Harbour—fill every vase I own, every vase my mother owns. They float in bowls. Single roses rise out of used wine bottles. An armful of them, deepest orange shading to palest peach, huddle together in the ice bucket.

My mother had to have helped him with this—or at the very least given him permission. Her rose bushes, as beloved as her grandchild, must have been stripped to the bare branches for this display.

I'm tempted to go out to the car and bring him back here, but I don't. It can wait. After the drive-in.

I take one more look around the patio, grab a green plastic jug and half a dozen of the purest pink roses and stop because I'm not sure I have the courage to do what I have to do next—walk out to the driveway and get into the car with my ex-husband, knowing what I know.

Or maybe that's not the problem. Maybe the problem is that I'm only guessing. If that makes any sense at all. Brad and I have not had a conversation about this, about anything even approaching this, all summer.

I can only hope that my dad and Rowena and T.J. have all been right. I can only hope that the woman in the rearview mirror is right and that I'm right. I hope that he wants me to ask the question. But I don't know. Not really.

The roses have made it easier. And harder.

The two pieces of clothing I'm wearing, the two pieces of clothing I'm not wearing—they were to have been both my question and my answer.

The roses have to be his answer now to the question I was too frightened to ask, to the question he's been waiting for me to ask all summer, maybe for all the six years we've been apart.

And I assume that I've answered it by saying yes to Hayden's trip to the city and, by implication, to the two of us alone at the Halfmoon.

The walk to the front of the house seems both endless and far too short. Brad will see everything the minute I turn the corner. He'll see my acceptance of his offer of the roses. He'll see by my clothing—and lack of it—that even before I saw the roses I knew what this evening meant and that I wanted it as much as he did.

He does.

He's leaning against the station wagon, arms folded over his chest, long blue-jeaned legs crossed at the ankle. His T-shirt is my favorite color—it might even be one I bought him—a deep midnight-blue to match his eyes.

He looks relaxed, but I can see the strain in his posture, the ever-so-casual look slightly out of kilter. His face is impassive, his eyes locked on me. I wonder if he, too, is unable to catch his breath as he watches me walk toward him and I wait to see his chest move, finally, as I reach the car and hand him the jug.

"Put these in the car," I say. "I want a reminder of what's waiting for us when we get home."

He smiles that definitely wicked biker smile that from the first moment I met him made me tingle. He takes the jug from my hands, careful not to touch my fingers.

I know why he's so careful because I feel the same way. If I touch him now, we'll never make it to the Halfmoon— we might not even make it back into the house.

We make the trip to the drive-in in silence. Me on my side of the big bench seat, he on his.

But I watch the muscles in his shoulders, his arms and hands as he drives, I enjoy the flash of sunlight on the golden hairs on his tanned fingers. I watch his thigh muscles shift beneath the denim as he applies the gas or touches the brakes.

Much of the time, his perusal of me is more subtle than mine of him, but only because he has to keep his eye on traffic. I see his nostrils flare when I run my fingers through my hair, releasing a wave of my perfume into the already rose-scented air.

I see his fingers tighten on the wheel when I shift in my seat and I swear that I can feel his body temperature rise when I unbutton another button on my shirt.

These are games we've played for years.

The Halfmoon is not too busy on this second-to-last Saturday night. It's Labor Day weekend, so there are tourists, but it's the final weekend before school starts and lots of locals are out of town getting ready for September.

But for my family this Saturday has always been a ritual outing.

It feels odd to be here alone with Brad, odd and frightening in the best kind of way. And I wonder, just for a moment, if this combination is what he feels when he gets on the plane to go to Kenya or Malaysia or some other country he's never been to before.

Anticipation, certainly. And a tingle of fear heightening his senses?

If what he feels on those trips is anything close to this,

I can see why he didn't want to give it up, why he wanted to share it with me and Hayden.

It's exhilarating.

We're early enough to get the far-left corner in the back row. It's not dark yet and won't be for at least an hour.

Anticipation.

Brad turns in his seat to pull a bottle of wine from the cooler, and I watch his body lift and stretch. I know this isn't part of the game, but I can't help myself.

I touch his back as he leans over the seat, my palm flexing on his body. I feel the muscles beneath my hand jerk and then settle and I hear the harsh breath he takes.

"Don't," he says. "Not yet. I can't bear it."

And I smile, pat his back one more time and sit demurely back on my side of the car.

The wine makes the conversation easier, as does the fact that we're sitting in my parents' station wagon looking out the window at the cars pulling into the drive-in in front of us. We've got something to talk about.

"There's Rowena," Brad says. "Who's that with her?"

I peer over at the black Porsche Boxster two rows in front of us. "I don't recognize him. Could be anybody."

"Yeah, but I'm going to drop in at the Way-Inn and see if I can find out who." Brad's always had a soft spot for Rowena Dale and he's a guardian at heart.

We talk about everything and nothing while we wait

for the movie to start. That's not what we're waiting for, but both of us pretend it's the movie and not the darkness.

"There's Hayden's teacher from last year. Remember? You met her at the open house. She just had a baby. She's on maternity leave this year. There's the sergeant and Julie—they're getting married in a couple of weeks."

I have an invitation to the wedding. One for me and escort, and one for Hayden. Do I ask Brad? God, here I am sitting in the car, sans underwear, and I can't ask him if he's going to be around in two weeks?

The woman in the rearview mirror appears, not in her usual location—that's angled toward Brad—but in the mirror outside my window.

You ask him. Now. There is no babying me, no suggesting that it might be a good idea.

And she's right.

"Brad?"

He turns to me as if he knows the tenor of this conversation is changing, though I try to keep my question as casual as it's possible to be when my heart is pounding and my hands are shaking.

"I have an invitation to their wedding. It's a couple of weeks from now, but if you're going to be around…"

Casual, yes. Obvious, also yes.

"I'm staying," he says. "Permanently." And he turns back to watching the moviegoers.

I wonder if he's been waiting to say those three words all summer. I wonder if they've been locked in his throat, waiting for me to ask him a question, any question, so he could use those words as a response.

But it's appropriate that he's used them here.

A sign.

The woman in the rearview mirror winks at me and disappears.

The sky darkens. The trailers begin.

I pretend to watch them, making the appropriate comments.

"I'd like to see that movie—I love (insert name of actor or director here). Hayden would like that. It looks like fun."

Brad doesn't say much of anything. I've always been a babbler when I'm nervous; he is the opposite.

The sky darkens further, the other moviegoers settle into their cars after trips to the concession stand, the movie—*Pirates of the Caribbean*—begins.

As always, Brad waits for me to make the first move.

He is taut with anticipation, as am I. The tension in his body thrills me and I take a deep breath before I move. I smell the roses, the scent of Brad's aftershave, the salty taste of ocean underlying everything. I smell desire.

And then I move, shifting to sit next to him, our thighs touching, his hot even through the denim. It's like my dream—but it isn't.

It's better.

Because Brad doesn't play by the rules.

He doesn't put his arm over my shoulder, he doesn't begin the spiral dance of passion we've perfected over the years, doesn't take it easy and slow.

He grabs me as if he's drowning and shifts us both in the seat until we're lying flat on the bench. And then he kisses me, kisses me until my lips sing, kisses me until I can't breathe, can't move, can only respond.

He kisses me as if he can't stop, and I kiss him back, our lips locked together as if they might never come apart. And I don't want them to.

I clutch his shoulders, his back. Wrap myself around him so he can't move, can't leave me again. And Brad does the same. His long, lean body is wrapped around mine, his hands touching me everywhere.

And we kiss as if we've only this one moment to make up for six years.

There is no subtlety in this car, on this night. No game playing. There is only longing and passion and a taste of sorrow at what we've missed.

"Enough," Brad moans, pulling himself up. "We can't do this here. We have to go home."

I kiss him one more time and sit up, straightening my clothes. I kiss him again.

"Let's go home."

And just like that, with that one sentence, I understand how I'm going to live without the Halfmoon.

CHAPTER 34

Coming Home

The drive home from the Halfmoon is as filled with anticipation as was the drive there, but the change is obvious. There are no more questions—all of them have been asked and answered.

I sit next to Brad, our hands entwined on my lap. Our bodies touch, hips, shoulders, thighs, hands, but it's more than that.

"It's been a long summer," Brad says. "I wasn't sure you'd ever see me, see why I was here."

"Oh, I saw you, but it took Dad and Rowena—" *and the woman in the rearview mirror,* I think "—to convince me to take the risk that you still wanted me, to tell me that the reason you were here was to force me to ask you if you wanted to stay.

"I was scared," I say, "because what if I asked and you didn't? For six years I've missed you, loved you, wished I hadn't been so stupid."

He looks at me and I have to blink away the tears. Because what I see in his eyes is a longing as vast as the oceans that have separated us for those six years.

But what he says is simple. "It doesn't matter. Not now. We'll work this out because we have to. Because I can't live without you or Hayden. Because my life without you isn't really a life at all."

It's amazing how a few hours can change your life, how the simplest of words can make everything right. I know it's not going to be easy. Families aren't easy. But they're worth it.

I touch his cheek, scared to go any further while we're driving. This thing between us is so explosive, if I kiss him now, we're likely to be arrested for indecent exposure. So I settle for the touch, the feel of his hand in mine.

We'll be home soon.

As we walk through the house, we turn off all the lights. The one on the front porch, the ones in the kitchen. We remove the night-lights from their sockets. Brad runs up the stairs and switches off all the lights I'd left on in my hurry to get to him.

I walk through the garden to the studio to turn off the motion sensors that flood the backyard with light if someone gets near in the night. I unplug the lanterns that weave through the trees.

The yard and the patio are dark and so is the house next to us. My neighbors are away for the weekend.

Crickets sing in the bushes. A warm breeze hums through the trees. All I smell are roses. *Roses and love*, I think. Roses and passion and the future.

Brad hands me a glass of wine and lowers himself down to the blankets I've layered over the grass. I take a sip, as does he.

I'm trying to be patient, really I am, but it's not working. Wine is *not* what I want.

I take Brad's glass and set it on the grass with mine. A moment of hesitation, but only a moment, and I turn to him.

This, too, is better than my dream. Infinitely better.

There are plenty of reasons for that, and I try to enumerate them while being completely distracted by Brad's hands on me, in my hair, on my breasts and my stomach and my thighs.

There's room here on these blankets in the grass. Room to settle into, to relax into.

There is no possibility of spectators here in our backyard. There is only Brad. There is only me. And the darkness.

There is quiet here, peace and stillness and silence.

There is no time limit in this place. There is no intermission, no movie ending.

There are roses here, dozens and dozens of roses, laying their sweet summer scent over us.

And there is the future here on these blankets with us—our future—and that makes it more than my dream could ever be, more than I could have imagined six weeks ago, standing in my kitchen, the phone in my hand and Brad saying, "I'm going to stay all summer."

Our clothes, the four pieces we wear between the two of us, fall from our bodies as if they were soap suds in the shower, as if they were leaves in October, as if they were never meant to come between us.

And we're here, the two of us, naked and together in the dark.

Brad's skin tastes like my favorite things. Like margaritas on the beach in the hot sun of August. Like salmon steaks done perfectly on the barbecue—just lemon, salt, pepper and the taste of smoke underneath. Like cotton candy at the craft fair or raspberries fresh from my father's garden.

And I taste every inch of his flesh, as he does mine. We have time here in the darkness and we take it. But we're not playing games, not now.

We're learning each other again, which places to touch, taste and suckle.

My breath catches in my throat when he laps at my belly button and I hear his breath stop when my tongue touches the back of his knee. My breathing grows ragged when he moves lower, my body squirming beneath his, reaching for more, always more.

He moans when I push him onto his back and straddle him, moans again when I lower myself softly, slowly, onto him.

"Don't move," I whisper. "Don't move."

And he doesn't, though I know it isn't easy. I see the tension in his face, the passion now driving him hard. But he doesn't move, lets me set the pace, lets me pleasure him.

His hands on my breasts, his thumbs stroking my nipples. And then his hands in my hair, bringing me down to him, slowing me even further. He wraps his arms around me, holds me against him, no movement except the quivering of our bodies, and he kisses me.

He kisses me as if he'll never stop, and I feel the heat and I can't help myself. I rip myself from his hands and I move, pounding harder and harder, because I can't wait, can't stand the waiting, not one more minute. And I have my hands on his shoulders so he can't move and I pound against him, hotter and hotter until finally the heat explodes into flame.

But now he won't let me stop, won't let me collapse. He bucks beneath me, and now it's his turn to push, to push deeper and deeper until I can feel him so deep inside me it's as if we're one person. And the explosion this time is both of us, our bodies more than flame, more than together, better than anything.

Hours pass and the late-summer air grows cooler,

soothing our heated bodies. Brad rolls over, pulling me on top of him, murmuring, "Upstairs?"

And I nod yes, feeling his heart beating beneath my cheek, and I can't even think, not now. Maybe not ever.

He carries me up the stairs and into my room. "Our room," I whisper as he turns to get through the door. "Our room," I say into his ear. "Our house," I say as he lays me on the bed and follows me down.

"Mine," he says, kissing me. "Mine."

CHAPTER 35

Last Night at the Halfmoon

It's almost noon when we finally make it out of bed and down the stairs.

"They won't take the nine-o'clock, probably not even the eleven," I say when Brad first looks at the clock next to the bed. "We've got plenty of time."

The second time he looks at the clock, it's almost eleven. "Now," he says, "we have to get out of bed. Right this minute."

And we do, though sharing the shower—"To save time," he says with a grin—adds a few extra minutes to the plan.

I wonder if both of us are trying to make up for six years' abstinence in one night. If we'll ever get over this instant on switch we seem to have between us now.

"As long as we're downstairs by noon, then. Okay?"

"Race you down the stairs." I giggle, dressed and thinking about the clothes and wine and flowers on the patio. "Have to pick up the clothes at least," I say, "before the rest of them get home."

Hurrying down the stairs, Brad one step behind me, we arrive in the kitchen at the break of noon.

Mom and Dad and Hayden are sitting at the table, two coffees and one milk in front of them. The three of them are wearing masks—and these aren't the expressionless masks I expect Mom and Dad to be wearing in these circumstances, a mask I'm not sure Hayden could pull off, anyway.

No, Mom is wearing Minnie Mouse, Dad Porky Pig and Hayden a Darth Vader mask. And I know, damn it, it's perfectly obvious, all three of them are laughing their fool heads off under those masks.

"Where are Dad's books?" I ask.

Because I want to make sure that they didn't just take this trip and come back on the early ferry to put Brad and me in a place where we would be unable to resist the pull of each other.

"We dropped them off at home."

"Yeah," Hayden adds. "We just got here."

And I know that Mom's coached him on that because the grin on his face threatens to ruin forever his evil-twin disguise. It even ruins the Darth Vader mask he's wearing, because I swear that Darth Vader never looked so happy. Not even when he was dying.

I take a quick peek out at the patio, which, of course,

Mom catches me doing and she points at the bag at her feet. I nod my thanks and hope that she picked up our clothes before Dad or Hayden made it around the corner.

No way of being sure about that, though. No way of knowing how much they know, how much of this they've planned.

Brad's grin is as big as Hayden's as he sits down on a stool at the counter and reaches for the coffeepot.

"Coffee, angel?" he asks, cool as you please.

I glare at him, but he ignores me and Hayden giggles. Mom's giggling under her Minnie Mouse mask, and I expect Dad is, too.

"Coffee. Yes."

And I sit down at the table between my mother and my father because I know I can't sit next to Brad. It isn't safe. The raw desire on his face must reflect mine. It's definitely not safe.

Hayden reaches under his chair and pulls out two more masks. "Here, Mom, this one's for you."

It's not funny. I'm not laughing. I press my lips together and pinch the skin on the back of my hand. *Do not laugh, Aimee.* Nothing works.

I grab the Princess Leia mask and put it on over my giggles, lifting it up to drink my coffee, and laugh again when Brad puts on his Han Solo mask and grabs my hand.

"My princess," he says, laughter in his voice. And

turning solemn when he says, right in front of all of them, "Marry me?"

"What? You mean we aren't already?"

Everyone in the kitchen giggles and pretends that there's nothing unusual about a Sunday morning spent sitting in the kitchen wearing masks, nothing unusual at all about Brad asking the mother of his child to marry him, nothing unusual at all about finding our clothes in the backyard.

And maybe there isn't.

Maybe this is the way it was meant to be.

THE WEEK FLIES BY. Studio. Shopping. School. Packing. Shipping.

I don't have time to talk to T.J. more than to tell her that Brad's staying. Don't have time to talk to Brad about what we're going to do, though that doesn't matter—I know we'll work it out and so does he.

Don't have time to worry about the Halfmoon. Don't have time to plan anything for the last night.

But Saturday afternoon rolls around and Brad and Mom have everything set.

The station wagon sits in my driveway packed to the brim with food and drinks and people. When I show up five minutes late, my mother scolds me.

"We can't be late, you know. It's the last night."

"I know, I know. I'm sorry. I just had something I had to do this afternoon."

I show her and T.J., discreetly, the small velvet-covered box I have in my hand. Mom nods and whispers to my father sitting next to her.

He turns to Brad. "I forgot that one bag," he says. "Can you grab it from the patio?"

Brad looks a little confused—I'm sure he checked the patio before he got into the car—but he gets out without comment.

I touch his arm to stop him when he reaches me and take a deep breath to steady my nerves.

The box is midnight-blue—the same color as his eyes, I realize when I look down at it in my hands. He smiles at me and my nerves are gone.

"I saved this for you," I say, opening it and taking out his wedding ring. "And I saved this for me," I say, taking out mine. "I'd like…"

He doesn't let me finish the sentence, doesn't care that Mom and Dad and T.J. and Hayden are staring at us, doesn't care that we'll be late for the drive-in.

He puts his arms around me, lifts me up and spins me, faster than in the spinning chair, and I'm dizzier than the chair can make me no matter how fast I spin.

Because now I'm not spinning by myself. I'm not spinning for answers, I've got them. All of them.

BECAUSE WE'RE LATE to the Halfmoon, we end up in the front row, off to the side. But this night it doesn't matter. We don't care about the movie and I realize that we never really did.

Nights at the Halfmoon were never about the movies. They were always about the company.

My parents, my best friend, my wonderful no-longer-sullen Hayden and the love of my life. This is what the Halfmoon is all about, and it doesn't matter that this is the last night because I'll take home with me what has always mattered here.

MOVIES AT THE HALFMOON

La Dolce Vita (The Sweet Life) 1960 Federico Fellini, Director; Marcello Mastroianni, Anita Ekberg, Anouk Aimée

On the Waterfront 1954 Elia Kazan, Director; Marlon Brando, Karl Malden, Lee J. Cobb, Rod Steiger

Long Day's Journey Into Night 1962 Sidney Lumet, Director; Katharine Hepburn, Ralph Richardson, Jason Robards, Dean Stockwell

Lord of the Rings: The Fellowship of the Ring 2001 Peter Jackson, Director; Viggo Mortensen, Ian McKellen, Elijah Wood, Sean Astin, Orlando Bloom, Liv Tyler

Lord of the Rings: The Two Towers 2002

Quest for Fire 1981 Jean-Jacques Annaud, Director; Rae Dawn Chong

The Piano 1993 Jane Campion, Director; Holly Hunter, Harvey Keitel, Sam Neill, Anna Paquin

Macbeth 1948 Orson Welles, Director and Macbeth

Star Wars 1977 George Lucas, Director; Mark Hamill, Harrison Ford, Carrie Fisher, Alec Guinness

Risky Business 1983 Paul Brickman, Director; Tom Cruise, Rebecca De Mornay

Dark Victory 1939 Edmund Goulding, Director; Bette Davis, Humphrey Bogart, George Brent

Sunset Boulevard 1950 Billy Wilder, Director; Gloria Swanson, William Holden

Gone With the Wind 1939 Victor Fleming, Director; Clark Gable, Vivien Leigh, Leslie Howard, Olivia de Havilland

Superman Returns 2006 Bryan Singer, Director; Brandan Routh, Kate Bosworth

Six Degrees of Separation 1993 Fred Schepisi, Director; Stockard Channing, Will Smith, Donald Sutherland

Pinocchio 1940, Disney

The Prince of Tides 1991 Barbra Streisand, Director; Barbra Streisand, Nick Nolte

Wall Street 1987 Oliver Stone, Director; Charlie Sheen, Martin Sheen, Michael Douglas

Easy Rider 1969 Dennis Hopper, Director; Dennis Hopper, Peter Fonda, Jack Nicholson

Hello, Dolly! 1969 Gene Kelly, Director; Barbra Streisand, Walter Matthau

The Cat in the Hat 2003 Bo Welch, Director; Mike Myers

The Man in the Iron Mask 1998 Randall Wallace, Director; Leonardo DiCaprio, Jeremy Irons, John Malkovich, Gerard Depardieu, Gabriel Byrne

Pirates of the Caribbean: Dead Man's Chest 2006 Gore Verbinski, Director; Johnny Depp, Orlando Bloom, Keira Knightley

The Pink Panther 1963 Blake Edwards, Director; Peter Sellers

War of the Worlds 2005 Steven Spielberg, Director; Tom Cruise

Star Wars: Attack of the Clones 2002 George Lucas, Director; Ewan McGregor, Natalie Portman, Hayden Christensen, Samuel L. Jackson

Lord of the Rings: Return of the King 2003

Monsters, Inc. 2001, Pete Docter, David Silverman, Directors; John Goodman, Billy Crystal

The Tango Lesson 1997 Sally Potter, Director; Sally Potter

Le Divorce 2003 James Ivory, Director; Kate Hudson

The Poseidon Adventure 1972 Ronald Neame, Director; Gene Hackman, Ernest Borgnine, Shelley Winters

Big Night 1996 Campbell Scott, Stanley Tucci, Directors; Stanley Tucci, Tony Shalhoub

Ice Age: The Meltdown 2006 Carlos Saldanha, Director; Ray Romano, John Leguizamo, Denis Leary, Queen Latifah

Days of Wine and Roses 1962 Blake Edwards, Director; Jack Lemmon, Lee Remick, Jack Klugman

Who's Afraid of Virginia Woolf? 1966 Mike Nichols, Director; Elizabeth Taylor, Richard Burton

Gidget Goes Hawaiian 1961 Paul Wendkos, Director; James Darren, Deborah Walley

Eat Drink Man Woman 1994 Ang Lee, Director

The Lawnmower Man 1992 Brett Leonard, Director; Jeff Fahey, Pierce Brosnan

What's New, Pussycat? 1965 Clive Donner, Director; Peter Sellers, Peter O'Toole, Romy Schneider, Woody Allen

Something's Got to Give 1962 George Cukor, Director; Dean Martin, Marilyn Monroe

A Midsummer Night's Dream 1999 Michael Hoffman, Director; Kevin Kline, Stanley Tucci, Michelle Pfeiffer, Rupert Everett

Tequila Sunrise 1988 Robert Towne, Director; Mel Gibson, Michelle Pfeiffer, Kurt Russell

The Big Easy 1987 Jan McBride, Director; Dennis Quaid, Ellen Barkin

Sleeping Beauty 1959 Disney

Wings of Desire 1987 Wim Wenders, Director; Bruno Ganz, Solveig Dommartin

Coming Home 1978 Hal Ashby, Director; Jon Voight, Jane Fonda, Bruce Dern

Mediterranean Nights

Join the guests and crew of Alexandra's Dream,
the newest luxury ship to set sail on the
romantic Mediterranean, as they experience
the glamorous world of cruising.

A new Harlequin continuity series
begins in June 2007 with
FROM RUSSIA, WITH LOVE
by Ingrid Weaver.

Marina Artamova books a cabin on the
luxurious cruise ship Alexandra's Dream,
when she finds out that her orphaned nephew
and his adoptive father are aboard.
She's determined to be reunited with the boy…
but the romantic ambience of the ship and
her undeniable attraction to a man she considers
her enemy are about to interfere with her quest!

Turn the page for a sneak preview!

Piraeus, Greece

"There she is, Stefan. *Alexandra's Dream*." David Anderson squatted beside his new son and pointed at the dark blue hull that towered above the pier. The cruise ship was a majestic sight, twelve decks high and as long as a city block. A circle of silver and gold stars, the logo of the Liberty Cruise Line, gleamed from the swept-back smokestack. Like some legendary sea creature born for the water, the ship emanated power from every sleek curve— even at rest it held the promise of motion. "That's going to be our home for the next ten days."

The child beside him remained silent, his cheeks working in and out as he sucked furiously on his thumb. Hair so blond it appeared white ruffled against his forehead in the harbor breeze. The baby-sweet scent unique to the very young mingled with the tang of the sea.

"Ship," David said. "Uh, *parakhod*."

From beneath his bangs, Stefan looked at the *Alexandra's*

Dream. Although he didn't release his thumb, the corners of his mouth tightened with the beginning of a smile.

David grinned. That was Stefan's first smile this afternoon, one of only two since they had left the orphanage yesterday. It was probably because of the boat—according to the orphanage staff, the boy loved boats, which was the main reason David had decided to book this cruise. Then again, there was a strong possibility the smile could have been a reaction to David's attempt at pocket-dictionary Russian. Whatever the cause, it was a good start.

The liaison from the adoption agency had claimed that Stefan had been taught some English, but David had yet to see evidence of it. David continued to speak, positive his son would understand his tone even if he couldn't grasp the words. "This is her maiden voyage. Her first trip, just like this is our first trip, and that makes it special." He motioned toward the stage that had been set up on the pier beneath the ship's bow. "That's why everyone's celebrating."

The ship's official christening ceremony had been held the day before and had been a closed affair, with only the cruise-line executives and VIP guests invited, but the stage hadn't yet been disassembled. Banners bearing the blue and white of the Greek flag of the ship's owner, as well as the Liberty circle of stars logo, draped the edges of the platform. In the center, a group of musicians and a dance troupe dressed in traditional white folk costumes performed for the benefit of the *Alexandra's Dream*'s first passengers. Their audience was in a festive mood, snapping their fingers in time to the music while the dancers twirled and wove through their steps.

David bobbed his head to the rhythm of the mandolins. They were playing a folk tune that seemed vaguely familiar, possibly from a movie he'd seen. He hummed a few notes. "Catchy melody, isn't it?"

Stefan turned his gaze on David. His eyes were a striking shade of blue, as cool and pale as a winter horizon and far too solemn for a child not yet five. Still, the smile that hovered at the corners of his mouth persisted. He moved his head with the music, mirroring David's motion.

David gave a silent cheer at the interaction. Hopefully, this cruise would provide countless opportunities for more. "Hey, good for you," he said. "Do you like the music?"

The child's eyes sparked. He withdrew his thumb with a pop. "*Moozika!*"

"Music. Right!" David held out his hand. "Come on, let's go closer so we can watch the dancers."

Stefan grasped David's hand quickly, as if he feared it would be withdrawn. In an instant his budding smile was replaced by a look close to panic.

Did he remember the car accident that had killed his parents? It would be a mercy if he didn't. As far as David knew, Stefan had never spoken of it to anyone. Whatever he had seen had made him run so far from the crash that the police hadn't found him until the next day. The event had traumatized him to the extent that he hadn't uttered a word until his fifth week at the orphanage. Even now he seldom talked.

David sat back on his heels and brushed the hair from Stefan's forehead. That solemn, too-old gaze locked with his, and for an instant, David felt as if he looked back in time at an image of himself thirty years ago.

He didn't need to speak the same language to understand exactly how this boy felt. He knew what it meant to be alone and powerless among strangers, trying to be brave and tough but wishing with every fiber of his being for a place to belong, to be safe, and most of all for someone to love him....

He knew in his heart he would be a good parent to Stefan. It was why he had never considered halting the adoption process after Ellie had left him. He hadn't balked when he'd learned of the recent claim by Stefan's spinster aunt, either; the absentee relative had shown up too late for her case to be considered. The adoption was meant to be. He and this child already shared a bond that went deeper than paperwork or legalities.

A seagull screeched overhead, making Stefan start and press closer to David.

"That's my boy," David murmured. He swallowed hard, struck by the simple truth of what he had just said.

That's my boy.

"I CAN'T BE PATIENT, RUDOLPH. I'm not going to stand by and watch my nephew get ripped from his country and his roots to live on the other side of the world."

Rudolph hissed out a slow breath. "Marina, I don't like the sound of that. What are you planning?"

"I'm going to talk some sense into this American kidnapper."

"No. Absolutely not. No offence, but diplomacy is not your strong suit."

"Diplomacy be damned. Their ship's due to sail at five o'clock."

"Then you wouldn't have an opportunity to speak with him even if his lawyer agreed to a meeting."

"I'll have ten days of opportunities, Rudolph, since I plan to be on board that ship."

* * * * *

*Follow Marina and David as they
join forces to uncover the reason behind
little Stefan's unusual silence, and the secret
behind the death of his parents....*

*Look for From Russia, With Love
by Ingrid Weaver
in stores June 2007.*

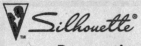

Silhouette®
Romantic
SUSPENSE

**Sparked by Danger,
Fueled by Passion.**

*This month and every month look for
four new heart-racing romances
set against a backdrop of suspense!*

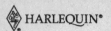
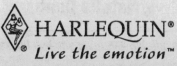

HARLEQUIN®

Super Romance®

Acclaimed author
Brenda Novak
returns to Dundee, Idaho, with

COULDA BEEN A COWBOY

After gaining custody of his infant son,
professional athlete Tyson Garnier hopes to escape
the media and find some privacy in Dundee, Idaho.
He also finds Dakota Brown. But is she ready for the
potential drama that comes with him?

Also watch for:

BLAME IT ON THE DOG by Amy Frazier
(Singles...with Kids)

HIS PERFECT WOMAN by Kay Stockham

DAD FOR LIFE by Helen Brenna
(A Little Secret)

MR. IRRESISTIBLE by Karina Bliss

WANTED MAN by Ellen K. Hartman

Available June 2007 wherever Harlequin books are sold!

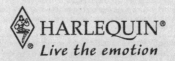

HARLEQUIN®
Live the emotion

REQUEST YOUR FREE BOOKS!

2 FREE NOVELS PLUS 2 FREE GIFTS!

There's the life you planned. And there's what comes next.

YES! Please send me 2 FREE Harlequin® NEXT™ novels and my 2 FREE mystery gifts. After receiving them, if I don't wish to receive any more books, I can return the shipping statement marked "cancel." If I don't cancel, I will receive 4 brand-new novels every other month and be billed just $3.99 per book in the U.S. or $4.74 per book in Canada, plus 25¢ shipping and handling per book plus applicable taxes, if any.* That's a savings of over 25% off the cover price! I understand that accepting the 2 free books and gifts places me under no obligation to buy anything. I can always return a shipment and cancel at any time. Even if I never buy anything from Harlequin, the two free books and gifts are mine to keep forever.

155 HDN EL33   355 HDN EL4F

Name _____ (PLEASE PRINT)

Address _____ Apt. #

City _____ State/Prov. _____ Zip/Postal Code

Signature (if under 18, a parent or guardian must sign)

Order online at www.TryNEXTNovels.com

Or mail to the **Harlequin Reader Service®:**

IN U.S.A.: P.O. Box 1867, Buffalo, NY 14240-1867
IN CANADA: P.O. Box 609, Fort Erie, Ontario L2A 5X3

Not valid to current Harlequin NEXT subscribers.

Want to try two free books from another line?
Call 1-800-873-8635 or visit www.morefreebooks.com

* Terms and prices subject to change without notice. NY residents add applicable sales tax. Canadian residents will be charged applicable provincial taxes and GST. This offer is limited to one order per household. All orders subject to approval. Credit or debit balances in a customer's account(s) may be offset by any other outstanding balance owed by or to the customer. Please allow 4 to 6 weeks for delivery.

Your Privacy: Harlequin Books is committed to protecting your privacy. Our Privacy Policy is available online at www.eHarlequin.com or upon request from the Harlequin Reader Service. From time to time we make our lists of customers available to reputable firms who may have a product or service of interest to you. If you would prefer we not share your name and address, please check here. ☐

NEXT07R

SPECIAL EDITION™

COMING IN JUNE

HER LAST FIRST DATE

by *USA TODAY* bestselling author

SUSAN MALLERY

After one too many bad dates, Crissy Phillips
finally swore off men. Recently widowed,
pediatrician Josh Daniels can't risk losing his
heart. With an intense attraction pulling them
together, will their fear keep them apart?
Or will one wild night change everything…?

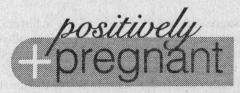

***Sometimes the unexpected
is the best news of all….***

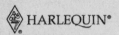

nocturne™

IT'S TIME TO DISCOVER
THE RAINTREE TRILOGY...

There have always been those among us
who are more than human...

Don't miss the dramatic first book by
New York Times bestselling author

LINDA
HOWARD

RAINTREE:
Inferno

On sale May.

Raintree: Haunted by Linda Winstead Jones
Available June.

Raintree: Sanctuary by Beverly Barton
Available July.

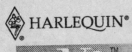

® HARLEQUIN®

COMING NEXT MONTH

#85 PRIME TIME • Hank Phillippi Ryan

In her debut novel, real-life Boston TV reporter
Hank Phillippi Ryan takes you behind the scenes of TV
news—its on-camera glitz and off-camera grit. *Prime Time*'s
heroine, Charlie McNally, is investigating the scoop of her
career—one that could lead to the man of her dreams…or
get her killed for knowing way, *way* too much.

#86 MADAM OF THE HOUSE • Donna Birdsell

With sales in the toilet and her soon-to-be-ex sucking her
savings dry, real estate agent Cecilia Katz and her handsome
assistant devise a very *special* open house—charging single
friends of a certain age to hook up with young men in need
of cold, hard cash. Can the makeshift madam close the
deal…or will this risky business be her downfall?

NXTCNM0507

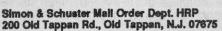